Sphinx

HENRIQUE MAXIMIANO COELHO NETO

Sphinx: A Neo-Gothic Novel from Brazil

Translated by

Kim F. Olson

Introduction by

M. Elizabeth Ginway

Afterword by

Jess Nevins

Modern Language Association of America

New York 2023

85 Broad Street, New York, New York 10004
www.mla.org

To order MLA publications, visit www.mla.org/books. For wholesale and international orders, see www.mla.org/bookstore-orders.

The MLA office is located on the island known as Mannahatta (Manhattan) in Lenapehoking, the homeland of the Lenape people. The MLA pays respect to the original stewards of this land and to the diverse and vibrant Native communities that continue to thrive in New York City.

Cover illustration: Ismael Nery. *Nós*. The Picture Art Collection / Alamy Stock Photo.

Texts and Translations 41
ISSN 1079-2538

Library of Congress Cataloging-in-Publication Data

Names: Coelho Netto, Henrique, 1864–1934, author. | Olson, Kim F., translator. | Ginway, M. Elizabeth, writer of introduction. | Nevins, Jess, writer of afterword.
Title: Sphinx : a neo-gothic novel from Brazil / Henrique Maximiano Coelho Neto ; translated by Kim F. Olson ; introduction by M. Elizabeth Ginway ; afterword by Jess Nevins.
Other titles: Esfinge. English
Description: New York : Modern Language Association of America, 2023.
Series: Texts and translations, 1079-2538 ; 41 | Includes bibliographical references.
Identifiers: LCCN 2023007003 (print) | LCCN 2023007004 (ebook) | ISBN 9781603296236 (paperback) | ISBN 9781603296243 (EPUB)
Subjects: LCGFT: Gothic fiction. | Novels.
Classification: LCC PQ9697.C42 E8413 2023 (print) | LCC PQ9697.C42 (ebook) | DDC 869.3/41—dc23/eng/20230223
LC record available at https://lccn.loc.gov/2023007003
LC ebook record available at https://lccn.loc.gov/2023007004

Contents

Introduction

M. Elizabeth Ginway

Kim F. Olson's translation of the 1908 Brazilian novel *Esfinge* (*Sphinx*), by Henrique Maximiano Coelho Neto, is particularly timely as it offers an international dimension to the increasingly popular field of gender and sexuality studies. I taught this innovative work in Portuguese in an undergraduate class on Latin American speculative fiction,[1] and my students responded with empathy and curiosity. They also expressed surprise that such a work, with its sympathetic treatment of the novel's uniquely transgender protagonist,[2] James Marian—the metaphorical "sphinx" of the title—could have been produced in Brazil at the start of the twentieth century. Like his protagonist, Coelho Neto remains an enigma, as his legacy in Brazilian literary history continues to be the object of controversy and curiosity (Gonçalves 26). It is interesting and fortunate that, after years of neglect, his works of mystery and the macabre are gaining new traction.

Coelho Neto and Brazilian Literary History

Conventional literary biographies portray Coelho Neto (1864–1934) as a successful Brazilian author, politician, and professor. A literary tour de force during the late nineteenth and early twentieth centuries, Coelho Neto published over 120 volumes during his lifetime, covering a wide range of topics, including Brazilian history, social and political conflicts, the rift between science and spiritism, and the divide between materialism and art. Despite a long list of successes, including a nomination for the Nobel Prize in 1932, his florid literary style and historical subject matter caused him to fall out of favor among readers and critics. As a result, Coelho Neto's works are now generally known only to literary specialists in Brazil.

To study Coelho Neto is to have a crash course in literary canonization and the politics of literary history. The author's stature has long been the subject of controversy: he was characterized as more of a "historiador" ("historian") than a literary genius by Brazil's greatest writer, Joaquim Maria Machado de Assis (Lopes 78; my trans.); later criticized as "nefasto" ("nefarious") by Lima Barreto; then lauded as Brazil's greatest novelist by Otávio de Faria (Bosi 75–76; my trans.). This ambivalent but mostly unenthusiastic view of Coelho Neto was solidified when Brazilian avant-garde poets and writers of the 1920s, known as *modernistas*, reevaluated national literary history and designated Coelho Neto and his generation of novelists as premodernist for their combination of nationalist themes and traditional (and often ornate) literary style. Brazil's iconoclastic *modernistas* celebrated the 1922 centennial of Brazil's political and cultural independence from Portugal by bringing a fresh, contemporary outlook to Brazil's artistic scene. Mary L. Daniel summarizes the *modernistas'* opinion of Coelho Neto's work by quoting the poet Oswald de Andrade, who quipped, "Não li e não gostei" ("I've never read [him] and never liked [him]"; 175; my trans.). Many modernist authors subsequently worked for cultural agencies in the Brazilian government or in publishing houses, where they became the predominant voices in determining Brazilian literary taste and canonization beginning in the 1930s and especially after 1945 (Johnson 20–21).

One of Brazil's most influential essays about Coelho Neto appeared in Alfredo Bosi's *O pré-modernismo* (*Premodernism*), part of a six-volume set on Brazilian literary history. Bosi alternately describes the work of Coelho Neto as "documental" ("documentary") and "ornamental" ("ornamental"; 75; my trans.), characterizations that have subsequently solidified into the general assessment of the author's work. After describing Coelho Neto's best-known novels and noting their principal focus—Brazilian history, rural life, and middle-class mores—Bosi makes passing reference to another feature of Coelho Neto's work, namely spiritism and the occult sciences, citing the novels *O rei fantasma* (*The Ghost King*), *O rajá de Pendjab* (*The Raj of Punjab*), *Esfinge*, and *Imortalidade* (*Immortality*; 79). Bosi classifies Coelho Neto as an example of a conservative premodernist, whose work he contrasts with that of more socially progressive authors such as Barreto and Euclides da Cunha (75, 77), both of whom continue to garner contemporary critical attention. The critic Massaud Moisés gives a similar assessment of Coelho Neto's work, calling it uneven in quality and noting that Coelho Neto wrote at such a furious pace that he had little time for editing (110), an assessment of Coelho Neto echoed by David T. Haberly in *The Cambridge History of Latin American Literature* (152). Significantly, many Brazilian high school textbooks exclude Coelho Neto from their lists of premodernists, perhaps for these reasons.[3] Aside from articles on *Sphinx* by M. Elizabeth Ginway ("Transgendering") and Daniel Serravalle de Sá, little has been published about Coelho Neto in English, with the exception of an entry in Irwin Stern's *Dictionary of Brazilian Literature* ("Coelho Neto" [*Dictionary*]), and Isaac Goldberg's 1921 translation of Coelho Neto's "Os pombos" ("The Pigeons") is to date the only English translation of the author's work (Coelho Neto, "Pigeons"). This translation is accompanied by an overview of the author's work, emphasizing Coelho Neto's treatment of racial oppression in *Rei negro* (*Black King*; see also Sá 77).

In 1993, the American critic Mary L. Daniel, writing in Portuguese, noted that renewed academic interest in Coelho Neto began in the 1990s when Brazilian publishers began to reprint his major novels, whereas before they had been reprinted mainly by the Chardron publishing house in Porto, Portugal, between 1903 and1928, with a few reprints by publishing houses in Rio de Janeiro.[4] A sign of this rekindling of interest is a 1997 study by Marcos Aparecido Lopes, which argues that there were few objective reasons for Coelho Neto's marginalization and that the oblivion to which the author had been consigned was due to arbitrary literary and cultural criteria (149). I would also argue that the true value of Coelho Neto's oeuvre has been inadequately assessed because of the critical emphasis on his historical and documentary works as opposed to his novels of the fantastic. Coelho Neto himself seemed to favor this part of his literary production, noting that in his youth he was influenced by Orientalist works, including *The Thousand and One Nights*, and imaginative Brazilian tales told at evening gatherings (Bosi 77). The emergence of the field of gothic studies in Brazil and a series of articles published on *Sphinx* have led to a renewed interest in Coelho Neto's oeuvre in recent years (Causo; Silva; Ginway, "Transgendering"; Santos and Brito; Garbo; Sá; Tavares).

Daniel, one of the few critics to offer a succinct overview of Coelho Neto's major works, divides them into four categories according to theme, and it is significant that none of these categories includes *Sphinx* or his other works of speculative fiction. The first category comprises his semiautobiographical trilogy about the abolitionist and republican movements, which includes characters based on historical figures and well-known intellectuals of the time. The three works that make up the trilogy are *A capital federal*

(*The Federal Capital*), *A conquista* (*The Conquest*), and *Fogo fátuo* (*Will o' the Wisp*; Daniel 175–76). A second category includes two novels of historical fiction that portray key events in late-nineteenth-century Brazilian history, including the declaration of the republic in 1889 and the naval revolt of 1893. These are, respectively, *Miragem* (*Mirage*) and *O morto* (*The Dead Man*; 176–77). A third category includes works that address Brazil's backlands and rural milieu, recognizing the struggles and historical oppression faced by the rural communities of northeastern Brazil and by Black Brazilians. Works in this category include *Sertão* (*The Backlands*), *Treva* (*Darkness*), *Banzo* (*Despair*), and *Rei negro* (175). The fourth, more general category into which Daniel divides Coelho Neto's work comprises texts that provide a panoramic view of Rio de Janeiro during the belle epoque, documenting the city's social diversity, contrasting the newly sophisticated downtown cafés, theaters, and shops with popular gathering spots such as gambling houses, spiritist centers, and the backyards of the city's outskirts, as seen in *Inverno em flor* (*Winter in Bloom*) and *Turbilhão* (*Whirlwind*; 177–79). Daniel comments on Coelho Neto's sensitive portrayal of women in these two novels, especially in his depiction of the decline of middle-class families, whose members descend into poverty, insanity, crime, and prostitution in the wake of the financial instability caused by a series of misguided government economic policies (177). Coelho Neto's work stands as an imposing monument of literary depiction of the outer and inner life of its author and the history of Brazil. It also captures a country in search of itself as it made a transition from the traditional institutions of the Catholic Church, the monarchy, and a predominantly rural society to new forms of thought and governance in a new, modernizing republic with a growing urban population.

Coelho Neto's Brazil

To understand the full implications of the historical context of Coelho Neto's life and work, we must recall that from 1822 to 1889 Brazil was a parliamentary monarchy whose economy was largely based on slavery and coffee exports. In contrast to other Latin American countries, Brazil did not fight a war of independence, because it had been the seat of the Portuguese Empire since 1808, when the court fled Lisbon before the invasion of Napoleonic troops. In 1822 the prince regent, Dom Pedro I, declared Brazil an independent empire and himself emperor. By the 1870s, increasing dissatisfaction with imperial policies on slavery led to the growth of the abolitionist movement and to the republican campaign that proposed to do away with slavery and the monarchy and establish Brazil as a new republic. A group of intellectuals known as the generation of 1870 adopted the positivist precepts of science and progress as the basis for reforms and became a driving force of cultural change, influencing Coelho Neto and many others of his generation. The chaos that ensued after the abolition of slavery in 1888 and the economic instability that followed the establishment of the new republic in 1889 deeply affected Coelho Neto's life and work. The First Republic was ruled by military leaders who engaged in repressive measures against the opposition (as in the case of the naval revolt of 1893) and attempted to modernize and restructure the Brazilian economy, though with little success, resulting in a stock market crash known as the *Encilhamento* (1889–93).[5] Governance was turned over to civilian rule in 1894, but the resulting policies proved to be just as brutal, as evidenced by the 1897 campaign against the peasant revolt in Canudos, in which some twenty to thirty thousand people perished at the hands of the armed forces acting in the name of the republic. Subsequent presidents returned the Brazilian economy to coffee production and other forms of early industrialization, including textiles (Silveira), without changing the structure of society in a profound way. At the same time, the politicians in Brazil's capital, Rio de Janeiro, undertook what they considered to be urban reform by clearing slums and undertaking public health campaigns. As Jeffrey Needell has noted in *A Tropical Belle Époque: Elite Culture and Society in Turn-of-the-Century Rio de Janeiro*, the transformation of the capital, complete with broad boulevards reminiscent of those in Paris and a new national art museum, a library, and a municipal theater, created a Rio de Janeiro with an elite European flair. As the social milieu of Coelho Neto's formative years, this sophisticated city later became the place of his work as a professor of art and theater.

The early bohemian years in Rio do not fully explain Coelho Neto's original approach to gender and sexuality in *Sphinx* or his play *O patinho torto* (*The Twisted Duckling*), especially given his traditional background and his place in the intellectual and political elite. His father, Antônio da Fonseca Coelho, originally from Portugal, emigrated to the capital of the northern state of Maranhão, where he married Ana Silvestre, a woman of Indigenous descent. After failing in business there, he moved his family to Rio de Janeiro. Here Coelho Neto grew up and attended a prestigious high school, Colégio Pedro II, where he met the future author Raul Pompeia, who would become part of a cadre of bohemians with whom Coelho Neto enjoyed an active intellectual and political life in the 1880s. Coelho Neto's mother and uncle were the driving forces in the author's life, encouraging him to cultivate his considerable intellectual gifts by pursuing higher education (Bourdignon 83–84). Although Coelho Neto considered a career in medicine, his distaste for the operating room led him to try law school. Moving to São Paulo to study law, he again met up with Pompeia and soon found himself involved in politics. Eventually, he abandoned his law studies to become a journalist in Rio de Janeiro in 1884.

Coelho Neto's circle in Rio comprised a number of important intellectuals, including the Black abolitionist and journalist José do Patrocínio, the Parnassian poet Olavo Bilac, the journalist Francisco de Paula Nei, and the naturalist authors Pompeia and Aluísio Azevedo, among others. Interestingly, two of these figures, Bilac and Pompeia, were involved in one of the most tragic scandals of the 1890s. In 1895 Bilac published an attack on Pompeia's political views that also indirectly referred to Pompeia's homosexuality, resulting in a challenge to a duel. Although the duel with Bilac was averted, Pompeia lost his job as the director of the National Library and subsequently took his own life on Christmas Day in 1895 (Miskolci and Balieiro 84). The historian James N. Green has explored the topic of homosexuality among the intellectual elite during the belle epoque, noting that it was an open secret that was tolerated but not immune to ridicule (*Beyond Carnival*). In 1911 both Bilac and the journalist and author João do Rio appeared in a cartoon in which they were shown admiring a Roman statue, implying that they were indulging in homoerotic fantasies (56). However, as Leonardo Mendes notes, there is no insinuation of Bilac's homosexuality in the two novels by Coelho Neto that portray his bohemian circle, *A conquista* and *Fogo fátuo*, in which the character Otávio Bivar is based on Bilac (141–42).

Coelho Neto reserved commentaries on sexuality and gender identity to his play *O patinho torto* and his esoteric and Orientalist-inspired novel *Sphinx*. In writing about the theatrical work, Alberto Ferreira da Rocha Júnior notes that Coelho

Neto includes a reference to a newspaper article about an intersex individual whose case came to light in the city of Belo Horizonte in 1917 (280–81). The text of Coelho Neto's play *O patinho torto* first appeared in a magazine in 1918 and revolves around the main character, Eufêmia, who at the end of the play announces that she will maintain a female identity for her mother at home but will otherwise adopt a male identity (Coelho Neto, *O patinho torto* 112). While Eufêmia's ambiguous sexual identity makes light of middle-class mores, the novel remains sympathetic toward Eufêmia and her desires, suspending moral judgment.[6]

It is hard to document the direct impact of the belle epoque and gender politics on Coelho Neto, since he wrote these works after marrying a woman, Maria Gabriela Brandão, who came from a traditional and well-connected family. As Renato Lanna Fernandes notes, Coelho Neto's father-in-law, Alberto Olympio Brandão, a well-known educator and local politician, helped launch Coelho Neto's academic and political career. A sophisticated intellectual and gifted speaker with family connections, Coelho Neto was named professor of art history at the Escola Nacional de Belas Artes (National School of Fine Arts) in 1892, and in 1897 he was one of the many supporting founders of the Academia Brasileira de Letras (Brazilian Academy of Letters), whose best-known founding member and first president was Machado de Assis. He became an instructor of literature at his former high school, Colégio Pedro II, in 1904 and was subsequently appointed professor of theater at the Escola de Artes Dramáticas (School of Dramatic Arts), becoming its director in 1910. He was also active in politics and was elected to congress as a representative from his native state of Maranhão, first in 1909, then again in 1917. In addition to these official positions, he continued to write for newspapers and magazines while also composing novel after novel as well as poetry, short stories, and theatrical works.[7]

In the 1920s Coelho Neto maintained his status as Brazil's most widely read author, and, despite the low esteem in which he was held by Brazilian modernists, he was elected president of the Academia Brasileira de Letras in 1926. Yet in 1922 misfortune had touched his personal life in the form of the accidental death of one of his sons, evidently moving him to convert from Catholicism to Brazilian spiritism the next year.[8] He continued to write into the early 1930s, but after his wife's death in 1931, he withdrew from literary circles, and he died in 1934, two years after his nomination for the Nobel Prize. As Rodrigo da Rosa Bordignon summarizes, Coelho Neto's life and work generally "expressam a conformidade com a ordem social e cultural estabelecidas" ("express conformity with the social and cultural order"; 96; my trans.), illustrating the idea that his life was generally conventional and not that of a crusader, despite his progressive views on gender.

As an intellectual writing at the turn of the century, a time of political turbulence, Coelho Neto alternated between the historical and the panoramic, on the one hand, and the esoteric and the intimate, on the other. And while few critics have emphasized his connections with the otherworldly and the hermetic, in this respect he could be compared to Spanish American modernist authors who turned away from politics to find solace in symbolist or other new religions, including theosophy. Borrowing from Neoplatonism, Pythagoreanism, and Eastern religions, theosophy also incorporated the Western idea of the spiritual evolution of the soul. As Rachel Haywood Ferreira demonstrates in *The Emergence of Latin American Science Fiction*, "noncanonical" science runs throughout the work of many Latin American authors of the late nineteenth and early twentieth centuries (133). These alternative sciences included mesmerism and magnetism as well as the religious practices of theosophy and spiritism (13–14). Luis Cano's *Los espíritus de la ciencia ficción* (*The Spirits of Science Fiction*) also argues that nineteenth-century works by Latin American science fiction authors take their cue from spiritism and the evolution of the soul as expressed in the works of the French astronomer Camille Flammarion while also including the aspect of adventure found in the works of Jules Verne (16–17). Thus, instead of depending on conventional science, technology, and outward conquest, as writers in the Anglo-American tradition do, Latin American authors relied on alternative forms of science and religion to focus on human relations, psychology, and inner or spiritual conquest in their own form of science fiction.

Other Latin American writers of the time also experimented with gender and spirituality, as Haywood Ferreira has shown in her analysis of the Mexican modernist author Amado Nervo's *El donador de almas* (*The Soul-Giver*), which tells the story of a male physician who shares his mind and body with a female spirit. Nervo's text depicts the physician Rafael Antiga as a lonely scientist who pines for a female soulmate. Rafael's friend Andrés Esteves uses his occult powers to provide one for Rafael, and the spirit, named Alda, enters the left side of Rafael's brain, hinting at a nonconforming gender relationship (Ginway, *Cyborgs* 88–89). However, the two characters maintain conventional cisgender roles despite sharing a male body, and although initially compatible, they eventually experience a falling-out and part amicably. Haywood Ferreira interprets the narrative as a disruption of the balance and pairing of opposites typical of Pythagorean thought, reinforcing the idea of conventional gender roles and the balance between male and female principles (169–70).[9]

Sphinx and the Neo-Gothic

Coelho Neto's novel of gender experimentation and the occult does not end as happily as Nervo's does, perhaps because of the embodied nature of James Marian's gender experience. Sá places the critical study of *Sphinx* within a line of gothic studies initiated by Ellen Moers's important 1976 essay "Female Gothic," which examines the role of the body and gender politics in Mary Shelley's life and works. The idea of an embodied gothic criticism was continued in a 1994 essay by Susan Stryker, who found the gothic approach to be expressive because it captures how medical sex reassignment can generate a naturalness of effect, yet such embodiment "places its subject in an unassimilable, antagonistic, queer relationship to a Nature in which it must nevertheless exist" (242–43; see also Sá 74). More recently, Jolene Zigarovich has applied the prefix *trans-* to the gothic because "it exposes trans characters and trans plots to underscore the genre's instability" (5). As Sá aptly summarizes, the gothic transgresses not only bodily borders but also geographic borders (74). This trans-gothic aesthetic accounts for both the content and the style of *Sphinx*, which crosses genre boundaries using a digressive narrative style that includes flashbacks, diary entries, poetry, and philosophical and religious speculation.

A key aspect of *Sphinx* is the transcultural exchange that results from the interactions between the English-born James Marian and the Brazilians with whom he resides in a boardinghouse in Rio de Janeiro (Sá 74). Here a variety of male boarders ranging from medical students and artists to retired bureaucrats and veterans gather at mealtimes to talk and to chat about other guests (Ginway, "Transgendering" 44). As such, the boardinghouse constitutes what Eve Kosofsky Sedgwick has called a "homosocial" space, one that is dominated by males joined by a camaraderie that includes homophobia (1). Although the boarders are mostly middle-class, single white men, some older, some younger, there are two female residents, both English: the motherly Miss Barkley, who runs the boardinghouse, and Miss Fanny, a young, red-haired teacher. A third English resident is James Marian, who has a robust physique and an uncannily feminine face. The novel is centered mainly on the mysterious identity of James Marian, whose nature is likened to that of the sphinx because of his queer or dual nature. In the Greek tradition, the sphinx has the lower body of a lion, suggesting masculine strength, and a female upper body, often portrayed with breasts, and a female head.

Roberto de Sousa Causo cites the Belgian Fernand Khnopff's 1896 painting *The Sphinx or the Caress* as a possible source of inspiration for Coelho Neto's *Sphinx* (115–16). In the painting, the sphinx is visualized as a type of femme fatale, a creature that is a portent or warning of things to come, representing both the fearsome and the sublime or otherworldly. At times, Coelho Neto's protagonist is evocative of gothic horror and recalls Julia Kristeva's concept of the "abject"—that which provokes a visceral sense of horror and revulsion, like that provoked by bodily excretions (2–3). At the same time, the fascination with the abject often makes it an object of curiosity. According to Judith Butler, this simultaneous sense of repulsion and fascination may extend to the social practices of certain groups whose rejection by society consolidates hegemonic identities (181–82). Although James Marian sometimes experiences this type of social treatment, his wealth generally insulates him from outright rejection, while his connections with the occult sciences afford him otherworldly powers.

In *Sphinx*, the unnamed narrator, a writer and translator who resides in the boardinghouse, discovers James Marian's secret when asked to translate the Englishman's diary. From this embedded text we learn that James was orphaned at an early age and taken to an estate to be raised by a housekeeper and a mysterious man named Arhat. At age thirteen, James is introduced to a boy and a girl—Maya and Siva—whom he befriends. Subsequently, when James finds the dead body of Arhat, he falls into a three-month coma. When he awakens, Maya takes him to a park where he meets the spirit of Arhat, who reveals that some ten years earlier, having learned of a terrible accident involving a brother and sister, he had used his surgical skills and the arcane arts (*magna scientia*) to save the body of the boy and the head of the girl by making them into a single being—James Marian. Arhat had introduced the two children into James's life in hopes of discovering the gender of James's soul but warns him that in either case he will always be an outsider. Some years later, having come into a considerable inheritance, James decides to travel the world.

Causo was among the first to explore parallels between Coelho Neto's James Marian and the monster in Mary Shelley's *Frankenstein*, characterizing both as artificial creations abandoned by their creators (113–15), although, to be fair, Arhat does attempt to offer guidance to his ward. Karen Garbo reads Coelho Neto's novel within the postcolonial framework of Gayatri Spivak's interpretation of Shelley's *Frankenstein* (98). Alexander Meireles da Silva places Coelho Neto's novel within the tropes of *Frankenstein* but emphasizes the role of the mad scientist over that of the monster (14), while Enéias Tavares places *Sphinx* in the tradition of the fantastic in Brazil, emphasizing the Freudian uncanny in his analysis of the novel (21). Naiara Sales Araújo Santos and Dayane Andréa Rocha Brito explore the history of gothic science, summarizing previous work on the novel by Causo, by Silva, and by Ginway ("Transgendering"). Finally, Sá emphasizes the idea of the artificial body in *Frankenstein*, which, stitched together (81–83), is a feature shared with Coelho Neto's James Marian, whose large neck scar marks him as a transgothic character.

A comparison can also be drawn between James Marian and Bram Stoker's Dracula, the title character of a late-nineteenth-century work of the gothic revival. Like Dracula, James attracts men and women alike, although his contact with them is mainly through conversation and unrequited love, while Count Dracula bites the necks of his female victims, suggesting penetration and sexuality. Although he is not predatory, James ends up seducing both men and women with his attractive appearance. However, James's seduction is almost inadvertent. The first victim, the teacher Miss Fanny, falls in love with him after listening to music with him in the garden. When James decides to spend more time away from the boardinghouse with a male friend, Miss Fanny's tuberculosis dramatically worsens, and she dies soon after. Notably, Miss Fanny's tuberculosis causes her suddenly to cough up blood, which connotes sexuality and violation, as if she were condemned to die for falling in love with this gender-fluid person. Later in the story, James characterizes his seductive effect on Miss Fanny as "[v]ampirismo espiritual" ("spiritual vampirism"; ch. 7).

Sphinx and the Queer

James's rejection of queerness and of Miss Fanny repeats his adolescent rejection of Maya during the years he spent with Arhat. In another interlude in Stockholm before arriving in Brazil, James lodges with a family and falls in love with his host's son but finds himself unable to continue with the relationship. He simply cannot live as a man or as a woman, preferring to remain alone and gender-nonconforming. Realizing the problematic nature of his love for others who are part of traditional society, he withdraws from the situation, as he did in his earlier life, and takes up his travels again. Mark De Cicco has used the polyvalent word *queer* to examine the role of the occult sciences in the literature of the Victorian period, when the term meant "peculiar" or "strange," "eerie" or "supernatural," or "transgressive," either physically or sexually (5). For De Cicco, the trajectory of the scientist-explorer who delved into the occult toward a space of the queer risked falling under its spell and possibly insanity. In his analysis of Robert Louis Stevenson's *The Strange Case of Dr. Jekyll and Mr. Hyde*, De Cicco notes that "the attempt to come to terms with the queer or abnormal, as well as the scientist's survival, depends upon the ability of the scientist to 'queer' himself and/or his subject in preparation for the encounter with the occult" (7). In falling in love first with a woman and then with a man, it is as if James Marian has developed a sort of immunity to his physical queerness, enabling him to live between two worlds and to embody both male and female traits, the physical and the mystical, without falling victim to madness or death.

Back in Rio de Janeiro, the text brings in elements of the supernatural. We learn, for instance, that James is able to produce ghost-like projections of himself. Shortly before Miss Fanny's death, James casts a mysterious spell on her and her fellow boarders, magically appearing before them, dressed in a tunic, while he is actually in another part of Rio interacting with others. Before she dies, Miss Fanny has another vision of James, and the narrator also states that he saw "James Marian e, naquele traje, o seu rosto realçava mais belo. Era ele, como eu o imaginara em devaneio" ("James Marian, and in that attire, his face was even more beautiful.

It was him, as I had imagined in my dream"; ch. 3). Here the narrator admits to seeing James's incredible beauty as if he had imagined him in a dream, suggesting an almost sexual fantasy. Another boarder, the musician Frederico Brandt, whose piano music charms both James and Miss Fanny, also confesses to having the same vision of a tunic-clad James floating in and out of sight near the boardinghouse. However, the musician likens James to an angel, a genderless being, emphasizing his androgynous quality. Miss Fanny's death is real, however, which leads us away from the spirit and back to the body and issues of gender identity.

Whereas James rejects his female admirer, he forges an intimate bond with the male narrator, who, as the translator of James's diary, knows his secret identity. Toward the end of the narrative, when James abruptly decides to leave, the narrator recounts a scene in which he dutifully returns the original manuscript to its owner. The moment would be banal were it not for the fact that, later, we learn that James had already left by ship the day before, making it seem as though the narrator hallucinated or experienced an uncanny, supernatural event. After learning about James's earlier departure, the narrator raves against Marian, claiming he felt possessed by a "súcubo" ("succubus"), a female supernatural being known for seducing men in their sleep through sexual activity: "Eu estava possuído, era uma vítima daquele demônio súcubo que me infiltrava na alma os seus sortilégios" ("I was possessed, a victim of that succubus demon whose bewitching machinations had wormed their way into my soul"; ch. 8). He subsequently suffers a mental breakdown from which he recovers only months later, awakening to find himself in an asylum. When a former boarder (and medical student) visits the narrator there, he offers a typical scientific explanation of the narrator's experience: namely, neurasthenia, the all-purpose malady of the overstimulated urban dweller. Here the narrative offers us a rational solution, leaving us with a Todorovian hesitation (41) between the natural (mental illness) and the supernatural (astral projection). This hesitation, I would argue, opens up a space for the topic of queer sexuality and gender nonconformity.

The Message of *Sphinx*

At first, the novel's aim seems to be to warn us away from the queer or the occult. Unlike Rafael Antiga, the doctor in *El donador de almas*, the narrator of *Sphinx* has not fully inoculated himself against the effects of the arcane arts and suffers a breakdown. We can extrapolate that, while Miss Fanny experiences physical death because of her desire for James, the narrator undergoes a type of psychological death or insanity brought about by his desire for the mysterious, sexually ambiguous protagonist. James Marian's character raises issues of repressed homosexuality and bisexuality as a threat to heteronormative society, evoking fears of degeneration that could undermine the values of Brazilian society at the turn of the century, as noted by the historian Dain Borges.

However, James Marian actually leads a privileged existence and is able to control his own life circumstances, lending him a more powerful spiritual, independent force. While his queer body may be perceived as a threat to some, his presence inspires a spiritual revelation in others. Coelho Neto may have been influenced by Kardecist spiritism, which found fertile ground in Brazilian society, where syncretic religious practices as well as popular Catholicism and Comtian positivism were popular among the middle and upper classes. The establishment of the republic and the separation of church and state allowed spiritism's doctrines of healing, charity, reincarnation, and karmic evolution to flourish (Hess 14–16) and to become a source of heated debate among Brazilians, some of whom saw it as a source of psychiatric therapy, while others feared that it would cause psychic harm. Alexander Moreira-Almeida and colleagues cite concerns by Brazilian physicians that spiritism provoked madness, noting that in 1909 a conference on the "Dangers of Spiritism" was held at the Medical Society of Rio de Janeiro, but no action was taken against the spiritist movement (9).

Although James Marian fails to find a sympathetic community among the conventional men of the boardinghouse, he serves as an inspiration to its artists, including the musician, the teacher, and the narrator, who is also a writer and translator. If physical contact is taboo for James Marian—as shown by his reaction to Miss Fanny—psychological empathy or creative inspiration are still an option for the musician and writer. Thus, James Marian's spiritual or otherworldly impact may reflect what Jack Halberstam has called a "delinking" from the "organic and immutable forms of family" (70), an attitude represented by artists and others open to new forms of knowledge beyond the traditional values of heteronormative society.

Coelho Neto's novel illustrates a fascination with the Orientalist thought that was popular at the time, and although this element is incorporated in a somewhat superficial way, it acts as a platform for commentary on Brazilian society from an outside perspective. This Orientalist strategy is also featured in Machado de Assis's story "As academias de Sião" ("The Academies of Siam"), in which a king and his concubine exchange bodies for a period of six months. By using an Asian setting to couch a discussion of gender ambiguity and the anxiety and violence that it provokes, Machado de Assis was able to critique the purported naturalness of gender roles and other conventions of his own society without threatening the regime of the Brazilian monarchy directly (Ginway, *Cyborgs* 76–79). Although the overt message of Coelho Neto's *Sphinx* appears to be a warning about James Marian's threat to established norms of behavior and traditional heteronormative morality, there seems also to be a second, covert message. As in the story by Machado de Assis, the theme of sexual ambiguity encourages readers to resist conventions and seek knowledge. This is the advice Arhat conveys to James in his final words before his death, telling him to use his fortune to bring enlightenment: "Faze com ele o que faz o sol com a chama: luz, claridade, calor, vida. O ouro da mina é o verdadeiro fogo da região maldita, fá-lo tu sol, luz celeste aplicando-o ao bem" ("Do with it what the sun does to a flame: light, clarity, warmth, life. Gold from the mine is the true fire of this cursed land. Make it your sun, your heavenly light, using it for the good"; ch. 6). In this sense, it seems that James is destined to bring out the hypocrisy of those who would otherwise shun him but accept him because of his money. His wealth grants him immunity from prejudice, allowing him to provoke others, defy convention, and open up new ways of seeing, despite the odds against him. Perhaps what is most remarkable about *Sphinx* is that it was written and published by a nearly forgotten Brazilian author whose imagination created an original contribution to global literature and gender studies.

Notes

1. Speculative fiction includes the subgenres of science fiction, fantasy, and horror. It should not be confused with magical realism, which is often associated with mainstream Latin American literature by Alejo Carpentier, Julio Cortázar, and Gabriel García Márquez, among others. See Haywood Ferreira for a discussion of this important distinction and the gothic origins of Latin American speculative fiction (8–11).

2. Coelho Neto's novel is an early example of speculative fiction that explores issues relating to gender identity. While it might seem anachronistic to use the descriptor *transgender* to refer to a character in a 1908 novel, James Marian's gender—articulated in terms of his masculine and feminine "almas" ("souls")—can reasonably be described as fluid. For more on gender and gender identity and for a definition of *transgender* in current usage, see "Gender."

3. Examples of high school texts that do not include Coelho Neto are Cereja and Magalhães's *Literatura brasileira* (*Brazilian Literature*) and Faraco and Moura's *Literatura brasileira*, which were originally designed to help students prepare for college entrance exams in Brazil.

4. A list of Coelho Neto's books—including two editions of *Esfinge* (original spelling *Esphinge*) published by the Portuguese press Chardron in 1908 and 1920 and *O patinho torto*, in *Theatro VI* (Chardron, 1924)—is available on the University of Pennsylvania's *Online Books Page* (onlinebooks.library.upenn.edu).

5. *Encilhamento* means literally a "saddling-up" and refers to the quick reactions of speculators to seize get-rich-quick opportunities that led to economic instability during this period and an eventual stock market crash.

6. Eufêmia remains a gender-nonconforming character throughout the play, according to Rocha Júnior (287), suggesting an openness to gender fluidity on the part of Coelho Neto, a view shared by Braga-Pinto (28). Published in *A política: A revista combativa ilustrada* (*Politics: The Combative Illustrated Magazine*) in Rio de Janeiro in three installments on 15, 22, and 29 November 1918, the published play apparently caused no scandal. For a discussion of the figure of the androgyne in *O patinho torto* and other works by Coelho Neto, see Braga-Pinto. Later, in the 1920s and 1930s, medical and political authorities became increasingly less tolerant of diverse gender expression; see Green, "Doctoring."

7. For a brief biography of the author in English, see "Coelho Neto" (*Acervo Lima*).

8. Spiritism developed in Brazil based on the teachings of the French educator Allan Kardec (pseudonym of Hippolyte Léon Denizard Rivail [1804–69]), who also held a doctorate in medicine. He is best known for his systemization of spiritist thought. Kardecism in Brazil is associated with spiritual evolution and esoteric thought and also includes homeopathic medicine and the practice of mediumship (Hess 21).

9. For an alternative interpretation of sexuality in the novel, see Ginway, *Cyborgs* 86–90.

Works Cited

Bordignon, Rodrigo da Rosa. "Coelho Netto: Homem com profissão." *Tempo social: Revista de sociologia da USP*, vol. 32, no. 2, 2020, pp. 79–100.

Borges, Dain. "'Puffy, Ugly, Slothful and Inert': Degeneration in Brazilian Social Thought, 1880–1940." *Journal of Latin American Studies*, vol. 25, no. 2, 1993, pp. 235–56.

Bosi, Alfredo. "O romance: Entre o documento e o ornamento." *O pré-modernismo*, by Bosi, Cultrix, 1966, pp. 73–89. Vol. 5 of *A literatura brasileira*.

Braga-Pinto, César. "O imaginário intersexual de Coelho Neto." *Novos estudos de CEBRAP*, vol. 41, no. 1, 2022, pp. 11–36.

Butler, Judith. *Gender Trouble*. 1990. Routledge, 2006.

Cano, Luis. *Los espíritus de la ciencia ficción: Espiritismo, periodismo y cultura popular en las novelas de Eduardo Holmberg, Francisco Miralles y Pedro Castera*. U of North Carolina, Chapel Hill, Department of Romance Studies, 2017. North Carolina Studies in the Romance Languages and Literatures.

Causo, Roberto de Sousa. *Ficção científica, fantasia e horror no Brasil, 1875–1950*. Editora UFMG, 2003.

Cereja, William Roberto, and Thereza Cochar Magalhães. *Literatura brasileira*. Atual, 2000.

"Coelho Neto." *Acervo Lima*, wiki.acervolima.com/coelho-neto/. Accessed 7 Oct. 2022.

"Coelho Neto." *Dictionary of Brazilian Literature*, edited by Irwin Stern, Greenwood Press, 1988, pp. 86–87.

Coelho Neto, Henrique Maximiano. *O patinho torto*. 1918. *Theatro VI*, by Coelho Neto, Chardron, 1924, pp. 11–147. *HathiTrust Digital Library*, hdl.handle.net/2027/inu.30000006693034. Accessed 7 Dec. 2022.

———. "The Pigeons." 1911. *Brazilian Tales*, translated by Isaac Goldberg, Four Seas, 1921, pp. 121–38. *Wikisource*, en.wikisource.org/wiki/The_Pigeons.

Daniel, Mary L. "Coelho Neto revisitado." *Luso-Brazilian Review*, vol. 30, no. 1, summer 1993, pp. 175–80.

De Cicco, Mark. "'More than Human': The Queer Occult Explorer in the Fin-de-Siècle." *Journal of the Fantastic in the Arts*, vol. 23, no. 1, 2012, pp. 4–24.

Faraco, Carlos Emílio, and Francisco Marto Moura. *Literatura brasileira*. Ática, 2000.

Fernandes, Renato Lanna. "Coelho Neto, Henrique." *CPDOC*, Fundação Getúlio Vargas, cpdoc.fgv.br/sites/default/files/verbetes/primeira-republica/COELHO%20NETO.pdf. Accessed 7 Oct. 2022.

Garbo, Karen. "O monstro possível no parnasianismo de Coelho Neto." *O inumano e o monstro*, edited by Ângela Dias et al., Dialogarts, 2020, pp. 91–103.

"Gender." *APA Style*, American Psychological Association, July 2022, apastyle.apa.org/style-grammar-guidelines/bias-free-language/gender.

Ginway, M. Elizabeth. *Cyborgs, Sexuality, and the Undead: The Body in Mexican and Brazilian Speculative Fiction*. Vanderbilt UP, 2020.

———. "Transgendering in Luso-Brazilian Speculative Fiction from Machado de Assis to the Present." *Luso-Brazilian Review*, vol. 47, no. 1, 2010, pp. 40–60.

Gonçalves, Márcia Rodrigues. *O Rio de Janeiro de Coelho Neto: Do império à república*. 2016. Universidade Federal do Rio Grande do Sul, PhD dissertation.

Green, James N. *Beyond Carnival: Male Homosexuality in Twentieth-Century Brazil*. U of Chicago P, 1999.

———. "Doctoring the National Body: Gender, Race and Eugenics, and the Invert in Urban Brazil, 1920–1945." *Gender, Sexuality, and Power in Latin America since Independence*, edited by William E. French and Katherine Elaine Bliss, Rowman and Littlefield, 2007, pp. 187–211.

Haberly, David T. "The Brazilian Novel from 1850 to 1900." *Brazilian Literature*, edited by Roberto González Echevarría and Enrique Pupo-Walker, Cambridge UP, 1996, pp. 137–56. Vol. 3 of *The Cambridge History of Latin American Literature*.

Halberstam, Jack. *The Queer Art of Failure*. Duke UP, 2011.

Haywood Ferreira, Rachel. *The Emergence of Latin American Science Fiction*. Wesleyan UP, 2011.

Hess, David J. "The Many Rooms of Spiritism in Brazil." *Luso-Brazilian Review*, vol. 24, no. 2, 1987, pp. 15–34.

Johnson, Randal. "The Institutionalization of Brazilian Modernism." *Brasil/Brazil*, vol. 3, no. 4, 1990, pp. 5–23.

Kristeva, Julia. *Powers of Horror: An Essay on Abjection*. Translated by Léon S. Roudiez, Columbia UP, 1982.

Lopes, Marcos Aparecido. *No purgatório da crítica: Coelho Neto e seu lugar na crítica brasileira*. 1997. Universidade Estadual de Campinas, MA thesis.

Machado de Assis, Joaquim Maria. "As academias de Sião." 1884. *Histórias sem data*, by Machado de Assis, edited by Afrânio Coutinho, Nova Aguilar, 1986, pp. 468–73. Vol. 2 of *Obra completa: Conto e teatro*.

———. "The Academies of Siam." 1884. *The Collected Short Stories of Machado de Assis*, translated by Margaret Jull Costa and Robin Patterson, e-book ed., Liveright, 2018.

Mendes, Leonardo. "Vida literária e homoerotismo no Rio de Janeiro de 1890." *Via Atlântida, São Paulo*, no. 24, 2013, pp. 133–48.

Miskolci, Richard, and Fernando de Figueiredo Balieiro. "O drama público de Raul Pompeia: Sexualidade e política no Brasil finissecular." *Revista brasileira de ciências sociais*, vol. 26, no. 75, 2011, pp. 73–88.

Moers, Ellen. "Female Gothic." 1976. *The Endurance of* Frankenstein*: Essays on Mary Shelley's Novel*, edited by George Levine and U. C. Knoeflmacher, U of California P, 1979, pp. 77–87.

Moisés, Massaud. "Coelho Neto." *O pequeno dicionário de literatura brasileira*, edited by Moisés and José Paulo Paes, Cultrix, 1980, pp. 109–11.

Moreira-Almeida, Alexander, et al. "History of 'Spiritist Madness' in Brazil." *History of Psychiatry*, vol. 16, no. 1, 2005, pp. 5–25.

Needell, Jeffrey. *A Tropical Belle Époque: Elite Culture and Society in Turn-of-the-Century Rio de Janeiro*. Cambridge UP, 1987.

Nervo, Amado. *El donador de almas*. 1899. *La revista quincenal: Revista literaria*, vol. 3, no. 5, 1920, pp. 3–79.

Rocha Júnior, Alberto Ferreira da. "Apontamentos e reflexões sobre as relações entre o teatro e a diversidade sexual." *O eixo e a roda*, vol. 26, no. 2, 2017, pp. 277–300.

Sá, Daniel Serravalle de. "Trans Gothic Double in Coelho Netto's Novel *Esphinge.*" *Doubles and Hybrids in Latin American Gothic*, edited by Antonio Alcalá González and Ilse Bussing López, Routledge, 2020, pp. 73–87.

Santos, Naiara Sales Araújo, and Dayane Andréa Rocha Brito. "Um olhar sobre os limites do corpo humano por meio de *Esfinge* de Coelho Neto." *Revista interdisciplinar em cultura e sociedade*, vol. 3, 2017, pp. 235–51.

Sedgwick, Eve Kosofsky. *Between Men: English Literature and Male Homosocial Desire.* Columbia UP, 1985.

Silva, Alexander Meireles da. "O gótico de Coelho Neto: Um diálogo entre as literaturas brasileira e anglo-americana." *Anais do V Congresso de Letras*, Universidade do Estado do Rio de Janeiro, São Gonçalo, 2008, pp. 1–22, www.filologia.org.br/cluerj-sg/anais/v/completos%5Ccomunicacoes%5CAlexander%20Meireles%20da%20Silva.pdf.

Silveira, Eujacio Roberto. "Indústria e pensamento industrial na Primeira República." 7ª Conferência Internacional de História Econômica e IX Encontro de Pós-Graduação em História Econômica, 15 June 2018, Universidade de São Paulo, Ribeirão Preto, www.abphe.org.br/uploads/Encontro_2018/SILVEIRA.%20INDÚSTRIA%20E%20PENSAMENTO%20INDUSTRIAL%20NA%20PRIMEIRA%20REPÚBLICA.pdf.

Stoker, Bram. *Dracula.* 1897. Edited by Nina Auerbach and David J. Skal, W. W. Norton, 1997.

Stryker, Susan. "My Words to Victor Frankenstein above the Village of Chamonix: Performing Transgender Rage." *GLQ*, vol. 1, no. 3, 1994, pp. 237–54.

Tavares, Enéias. "Androginia, sexualidade e monstruosidade: Uma introdução aos enigmas do/a *Esfinge* de Coelho Neto." *Monstruosidades do fantástico brasileiro*, edited by Cleber Araújo Cabral et al., Diologarts, 2020, pp. 10–25.

Todorov, Tzvetan. *The Fantastic: A Structural Approach to the Literary Genre.* Translated by Richard Howard, Cornell UP, 1975.

Zigarovich, Jolene. Introduction. *Transgothic in Literature and Culture*, edited by Zigarovich, Routledge, 2018, pp. 1–21.

Note on the Translation

The best way to get to know a city is by wandering through its neighborhoods and streets, a tremendous pleasure I experienced in Rio de Janeiro while living there as a young adult. Fond memories include visits to the old city center, home to streets such as Rua do Ouvidor and Rua da Candalaria, which I first glimpsed through bus windows while en route to obtain required identification documentation. To reach my destination, I had to ride along the famed beachfronts of the once aristocratic neighborhoods of Botafogo and Flamengo, no doubt gazing up at the palm trees lining the very real Rua Paissandu, home to the fictional Barkley Boardinghouse, the setting for Henrique Maximiano Coelho Neto's *Esfinge* (*Sphinx*).

It was against the lush backdrop of Rio's beauty that I encountered the challenges of this translation, which of course provides only one among a number of justifiable interpretations. To my knowledge, the book has not been translated before. Originally published in 1908, *Esfinge* is one of the few examples of horror in classic Brazilian literature from the first half of the twentieth century and has long been considered one of the great works of Brazilian science fiction. Coelho Neto's elaborate style was regarded as synonymous with the era's taste for the ornate, the sensual, and the fantastic. By making his descriptions as palpable as possible, he invited readers to enjoy the settings and their myriad pleasures, thus pulling readers into the thrills and horrors he presented.

The overarching challenge in my translation was preserving that authorial style and exoticism as much as possible so that readers of English could have the opportunity to experience similarly remarkable thrills and repulsive horrors. The difficulty was in rendering the English in a way that would eliminate artificiality resulting from what might be considered excessive sentence length and wordiness. I recognized that I had to walk a fine line between authorial voice and what I hoped would be finely honed evocative writing in English.

The antiquated spelling used in the 1920 edition (on which the translation is based), together with the esoteric vocabulary that is a part of Coelho Neto's flowery language, introduced an additional layer of complexity to the translation process, which required extensive terminology research, primarily through consultation of multiple monolingual resources in both Brazilian Portuguese and European Portuguese. There have been several spelling reforms and agreements in the Portuguese-speaking world, the most significant occurring in 1911, 1945, and 1990. The spelling used in the original, 1908 edition (the second edition, published in 1920, served as a basis for the current translation) was the spelling used prior to the 1911 Portuguese orthographic reform, which was the first time the language was standardized, ostensibly for the purpose of improving the literacy of Brazil's citizens. The main features of the revised system were intended to simplify spelling and to introduce principles of accentuation (Jones 168, 170).

My solution to these challenges involved careful consideration of word choices, which shifted my attention to the importance of precisely how the words were used. I had to determine which words were most appropriate to the early-twentieth-century time period, which words could serve as building blocks complex enough to mirror Coelho Neto's original Portuguese. As I moved through the process, I revised my methodology to include additional steps. In some parts of the novel, I painstakingly built the translation word by word, carefully choosing appropriate words that I pieced together to create full and often complex sentences. At times, I had to first decipher spelling before I could search for the meaning of a word. I found that archaic words were more readily located in European Portuguese sources, so I quickly learned to consult them first as a means of orienting myself. From there, I used Brazilian monolingual dictionaries, fine-tuning the English as I went along. Sections involving dialogue were particularly daunting because of concerns about the level of formality versus informality required in character exchanges. It was important to keep in mind that all but two of the characters are male and that characters range from university students to working professionals to retirees. It was also necessary to consider how best to present idiomatic expressions and the vernacular of the time in often heated exchanges. All the dialogue had to be sifted through the filter of usage appropriate to the time period.

Meticulous consideration of word choice was also part of an effort to reflect the many contrasts present in the text. These can perhaps be envisioned as concentric circles whose outermost ring includes the contrast between the larger worlds of the aristocracy and working classes in early-twentieth-century Brazil, between the spiritual and the corporeal, and between the lightness and heaviness of matter. Closer to the center are the contrasting forces of melody and discord as they pertain to man and nature as well as attraction and the many forms of repulsion. In the center is character development and its related contrasts, with particular regard to James Marian—male and female, emotional and physical, beautiful and repugnant—the result of an experiment involving both science and mysticism.

Imagine words that express the darkness and somberness of a 1908 funeral procession or the brightness and lightness of a Sunday game of *futebol* ("soccer") on a sunny beach that same year. Then imagine the darkness and brightness expressed through music and sounds, both natural and artificial. Numerous lines of the novel were given over to brightness—to the brightness of nature's music, present in the sounds of animals, insects, trees, flowers, weather, and bodies of water, and to the brightness of human artistry in the form of musical performances, poetry recitations, and assorted historical vignettes. Many were the lines written to express nature's darkness, heard through the tumble of rocks and debris, pelting rain, angry waves, wailing voices, and the cacophony of street sounds from carriages, streetcars, and early automobiles. But to best set the scene for the novel, imagine words that express the darkness of the haunting music of an organ, pounded out on a stormy night amid ghostly apparitions conjured up by troubled minds.

Work Cited

Jones, Maro Beath. "The Revised Portuguese Orthography." *Hispania*, vol. 4, no. 4, Oct. 1921, pp. 168–74. *JSTOR*, www.jstor.org/stable/331375.

Sphinx

I

The Barkley Boardinghouse on Rua Paissandu had the honorable distinction of a family home.

Inconspicuous and unpretentious, with nary a plaque on its granite gate, comfortably ensconced in a colossal old building, it seemed to sleep an enchanted slumber beneath the shadow of the palm grove in the back of the garden, where water trickled over pebbles, delighting the silence with a light and ever-present cool whisper.

Leafy arbors of jasmine and rose surrounded the tranquil quarters, and wrens, attracted by the peacefulness, calmly wove their nests among the mossy branches of the acalypha or cedar hedges, over which Miss Barkley, every morning at breakfast time, already corseted and the entire house in order, would slowly cast her gaze, of a mind that those fragile straw and feather alcoves also required her watch and ward. In addition to the main building, at the end of the acacia-lined pathway stood a small cottage, which the Englishwoman, in keeping with her somber taste and meticulous tidiness, had carpeted, furnished, and outfitted for Frederico Brandt, piano teacher, music critic, and composer extraordinaire.

It was in that retreat where the musician, able to devote only evenings to his study of the instrument since daytime hours were barely enough for lessons proffered in outlying neighborhoods, managed to lose himself in the classics and compose in the mysterious and nostalgic style of Grieg[1] when so possessed by genius, all without disturbing any guests averse to music, like old Commander Bernaz, with his rheumatism and his stash of Portuguese coins, who occupied the best rooms of the house, on the second floor, in front.

Miss Barkley achieved her miraculous order in godlike silence. A single gesture from her, a flash of her steely blue eyes, made all the brighter by her eyeglasses, would cause the servants to dutifully bow down, each intent on their duties.

If she happened to walk through the garden, gazing slowly around, the birds were said to chirp more restlessly and the roses to open even wider; the very water that normally trickled sparsely in a gentle flow would stream more loudly and forcefully in the damp shadow of the pteridophytes and caladium.

---

1. Edvard Hagerup Grieg (1843–1907) was a Norwegian composer and pianist and is generally viewed as one of the most important composers of the Romantic era.

She was a strong, handsome woman, lean and erect of carriage. Her smooth amber hair, drawn back into a bun, gave her cheeks added prominence. Her mouth was perennially rounded as if about to whistle, her pointed chin raised as if pulled up by the sharp hook of her nose.

She spoke little, and her severe demeanor seemed impervious to smiles.

Décio, a fourth-year medical student who often visited the pianist's quarters, scandalizing the boardinghouse with his unremitting high spirits, would call the well-groomed dried-up Englishwoman "a deformed male." But he extolled her acumen, the genius of her management, her puritanical austerity, and her learned worship of Tennyson.

A sturdy soul, seemingly barren, plain and weathered as a smooth-edged cliff, she was nonetheless worshipped in the neighborhood. At night, figures would stealthily pass through the garden, clutching their bundles—they were the underprivileged who had come for their daily ration.

More daunting than conquering a well-armed and supplied city was renting a room in that unassuming and modest house.

Miss Barkley preferred to let her rooms sit empty than to rent them out without the usual guarantees. She would carefully gather information by listening closely to potential boarders, her eyes sparkling as if afire as she shrewdly sifted through the intrigue, and only when fully convinced of their honesty based on evidence presented would she hand over the keys, with strict conditions of morality and a list of rules and additional charges.

Residence in the house was the greatest recommendation: a receipt from "The Barkley Boardinghouse" was as good as a guaranty in business and a certificate of good conduct in society.

Despite the manorial expanse of the building, only a few were lucky enough to enjoy its tranquility, the soft comfort of its overstuffed maple chairs, the fragrant whiteness of its linens, the dependability and abundance of its meals, and the flowers from its gardens that were fresh and ever-present on the dining table, on bookshelves, and in guest rooms.

Commander Bernaz occupied the hall and two rooms on the second floor.

The grumpy homebody with always a bone to pick spent the days indoors or, during the extreme heat, took advantage of the mornings and afternoons, dressed in his customary white linen suit and large straw hat, strolling in the shade of the garden with an old book in hand or settling under a pergola for a nap.

He was the most long-standing guest in the boardinghouse; some say he had advanced the funds to the Miss, the reason for her kind treatment bordering on sweet affection for him.

Miss Fanny, a teacher, had the room opposite Miss Barkley's—a spacious room opening out to the house's central area, full of flower vases, with a window to the garden. She spent her days outside the house, returning only late from her peregrinations through the neighborhood where she gave lessons to children, spreading the rules of English and instilling proper pronunciation, teaching history, geography, drawing, and music.

Constantly carrying her bag stuffed with booklets in English, whenever she saw a little one in some yard, she would call out and through the fence pass one of the compositions, showing them the drawings. Sometimes she would also distribute colored pencils and paperboard before briskly moving along.

On Sundays, she would corral chattering groups of children, taking them to the public gardens or the beach, where, happily laughing, cheeks pink and eyes sparkling, she would scamper about with them on the grass, through the trees or along the wet sand, giving them exercise under the sun while enjoying the wholesome emanations of the woods or the salty air of the ocean.

She was freckled and suffered from migraines and was never without a bottle of smelling salts and capsules in her bag.

At meals, she would speak English or begrudgingly mutilate Portuguese, grimacing as she fashioned the words in her mouth, as if they caused her nausea.

In one of the rooms that opened onto the veranda lived Alfredo Penalva, a rather temperamental fifth-year medical student, although one morning, the gardener found him stretched out and snoring under one of the arbors, clutching a bundle to his chest. When he lifted him in his arms, respectfully calling him to decency, the bundle fell out of his hands and came undone, and hard-boiled eggs rolled onto the gravel.

My quarters were on the top floor, near the stairs: a sitting room and a bedroom. In large chambers at the back of the house lived the widower Pericles de Sá, entrepreneur and Sunday photographer, and in front, filling the parlor and three other rooms, including the terrace, which was littered with jugs and pots of flowers like a Babylonian garden, lived the handsome and eccentric James Marian.

Yes, and I must be sure to remember Basílio the bookkeeper . . . he had an ascetic bedroom on the second floor, which was the source of never-ending despair for Miss Barkley because the man made a point of keeping it in much disarray, with books scattered around, newspapers and periodicals strewn on the floor. He would bellow if, when returning to his room, he saw his volumes in an orderly fashion, newspapers folded smoothly, periodicals neatly piled, and his pipes lined up on the shelf. He was once on the verge of moving out because Miss Barkley, in her desire for order, had placed an iron bookcase in the room, on which she had patiently, and gladly, arranged all his books.

In the basement in front lived three exemplary young men—one, a law student, Crispim; the other two, a pair of English brothers—Carlos and Eduardo—who were employed at an import company.

Miss Barkley was up each morning at five in winter, four in summer, and by six the house was resplendent.

The guests treated each other warmly except for the reclusive Apollonian Englishman on the third floor, who was always depressed and quiet and rarely came to the table at mealtimes, preferring instead to eat alone or in his room when not out in the garden at a small iron table beneath the acacia trees, his champagne chilling in a bucket as he listened to the birds.

He would leave the house early on Sundays, dressed all in white, carrying his tennis racket or bag of clothes for soccer.

He was in fact a handsome young man, tall and strong, straight as a rod.

But what was immediately surprising by contrast in this magnificent athlete was his beautiful feminine face.

His was a smooth and untroubled forehead adorned by gracefully hanging rings of golden hair, sad wide eyes of delicate blue, a straight nose, a small red mouth, and a round neck, white as a marble pedestal, that bore the head of Venus set upon the sturdy shoulders of Mars.

The Commander, who looked none too kindly on him, referred to him as "the Doll," and the always disagreeable Basílio could not stand him, thinking him ridiculous, with the face of a hairdresser's dummy.

James had arrived with excellent recommendations and baggage fit for a lord. Miss Barkley held him in high esteem, and at night, on the veranda, she would listen to him with delight as he talked about his travels to barbarian[2] lands, in caravans, dangerous hunts in the reeds of India, fighting with a Black tribesman in the Sudan, and all nature of adventure and recklessness.

He had traveled the world over. All that was left was to visit the frigid extremes of one of the poles, to hear the bears roar and reindeer grunt on the errant ice floe.

The guests were offended by James's aloofness and sardonic manner: they thought him ill-bred.

"Let him eat his pound sterling," the Commander would say. "No one is asking him for them. The brute!

2. The term *barbarian* historically referred to any individual who did not belong to the Greek or Roman civilization and who spoke a language other than that of the Greeks or Romans; a foreigner ("Bárbaro").

Not even a 'good morning' does he say . . . If he thinks he's dealing with Blacks from Africa[3] . . . he's mistaken!"

Miss Fanny would intervene, trying to keep the peace with her childlike voice and gibberish Portuguese. "He's different. A little embarrassed, shy . . . talk to him."

"Talk? To whom? To the Doll? Come on! For the love of God!"

One Sunday during dinner at the boardinghouse, Décio made mention of a handsome Englishman he had seen in passing.

"Imagine, if you will, the most beautiful head of a woman on the formidable trunk of a circus Hercules. Beauty and strength. The epitome of aesthetics!"

"Well, be aware, my friend," said the Commander, running his fork slowly through his potato salad, "under all that aesthetic, as you say, lies the biggest boor that ever was!"

"Do you know him?"

"Do I know him? He lives here!"

Décio's eyes widened as he exclaimed in a shout: "Here?"

"Yes, sir. Just ask Miss Barkley."

---

3. The original Portuguese, "negros da África," is translated literally as "Blacks from Africa." This usage is now considered highly offensive and old-fashioned. Given the boardinghouse ethos expressed earlier in the novel, the phrase might even have raised eyebrows among the characters.

Miss Barkley lowered her eyes, blushing. But there was one who dared challenge the Commander. It was Frederico Brandt.

"He's not a boor. He's just shy."

Everyone turned to the pianist as he helped himself to the fish.

"Shy?" Basílio exclaimed, arching his brow. "Why shy and not a boor?"

"Let me explain."

Miss Fanny put down her fork, curious, and all eyes turned to the dark face of the professor.

"One night, I was studying Beethoven's 'Pathétique' when I thought I heard someone out in the garden, cautious footsteps walking away. I ran to open the window, and when I looked out into the moonlight, I recognized Mister James.

"I stood there a little longer, admiring the night before turning back to the piano and playing late into the night. When I got up to close the window, he was slowly walking up to the veranda.

"After that night, he never missed my practices, and I play, certain that he is out there, somewhere among the trees, listening to me. He recognizes me and watches me. We run into each other every day. He has never spoken to me."

"He's a romantic," Décio explained.

"Arrogant!" sneered the bookkeeper.

"Arrogant, no. Shy."

Décio backed him up. "Perhaps. Generally, those behemoths are as shy and naive as children. Real strength is simple like nature."

"Oh, come now! Nature! Nature has no obligation to be polite. A man, yes, he should be well-bred. Of course, no one gets offended by the palm trees out on the street because they fail to make way for one to walk or shield one from the rain, but a man living among men has the obligation to be courteous. Now, a brute walking by me, stomping his feet without so much as a tip of the hat . . . that there, slow down . . . that's rudeness! I will not stand for it!"

"It's outrageous!" Basílio added, bursting into laughter. Pericles de Sá, who had been silent, cleared his throat. Penalva spluttered and coughed, and the two brothers, Carlos and Eduardo, beet red, used their napkins to stifle their laughter. Miss Barkley frowned in a pained manner, her eyes flashing toward the bookkeeper, who chewed purposefully. An uncomfortable silence hung in the air, interrupted by Brandt:

"I've done those things myself: talking only to those I know."

"What about him? Doesn't he know us? Doesn't he live here?" they all shouted, as angry as the Commander and Basílio.

"Yes, but . . ."

"But what? It's nothing but a bunch of hot air. You want to take the man's side just because he's going to listen to your songs. For God's sake!"

"I don't ask for an audience, Commander. When I want one, I announce a concert."

There was an awkward pause as the parties exchanged glances, embarrassed. Miss Barkley came to the rescue:

"Gentlemen, what an argument! What is this? On such a beautiful day? Really . . . Forget Mister James and his eccentricities. The English are like that; they have fog in their souls. Let him get some sun and you'll see him happy as a lark. Let's have our lunch in peace."

They were still arguing when the servant's bell sounded. The servant went to the third floor and returned to Miss Barkley with word that Mister James wished to have his lunch upstairs, with champagne.

The next day, a misty, windy Monday, Basílio, on his way down to lunch, came upon Miss Barkley in the hallway, where she sat at her writing desk behind a partition. The two exchanged words regarding the scene at the table the preceding day.

"You must understand, sir, I have young men here. I need to keep things respectful."

"You're right, Miss. I'm just hot-tempered, that's my nature. But there's no doubt about it. I'm never speaking to that man again: he is dead to me. And, look, tell Alfredo not to concern himself with my desk, just leave things as they are." He was forever defending the disarray.

One night, as I was writing, I heard what I thought was a moan followed by the thud of a body in the room of the Englishman. I kept on listening, and because the moans persisted I went out into the hallway and then to the door of the parlor. It was open, and there was a glimmer of light inside. The moaning stopped, and I was about to go back to my room when I saw Mister James appear, paler than ever, his huge eyes widened in an expression of horror, his mouth agape, his beautiful white neck bare down to the collar of his silk shirt.

He saw me and ran over, taking both my hands in his and dragging me over to the sofa, where he fell, panting. Stunned by the unexpected nature of the scene, I was unable to move as I watched him struggle, pulling at his shirt collar to loosen it, shaking his head in distress as he gasped for breath.

Suddenly, turning his beautiful big eyes upon me, he smiled with a feminine sweetness, opening his arms wide as he reclined against the sofa and relaxed his unsettled golden head.

I checked his pulse—it was racing; I touched his forehead—it was cold as ice. I sat down next to him and asked, "How do you feel?"

He stirred and stretched out his legs, his teeth chattering.

On the table was a bottle of whiskey and some glasses. I poured a drag, adding water, and offered it to him. He sipped it slowly. He sat there awhile, motionless, with his eyes closed, breathing heavily as if asleep, but little by little, calmness returned, and smiling with joy, murmuring words unclear, he began to rub his chest with his hand. He jumped up and very gently, very affectionately shook my hand: "Thank you . . . Thank you . . . !" He held my hand for a moment, wordlessly, finally letting go, and began to walk across the room until he reached the edge of the terrace, when he turned back hesitantly, staring at me with a smile.

I said goodbye, offering to do anything else he might need. He accompanied me to the doorway, grateful, explaining that he "was prone to some dizziness." He shook my hand effusively, smiling: "Thank you! Thank you!"

I retired to my quarters and that night was unable to make any progress on my work. I smoked at the window, read, and reclined, but sleep eluded me in my worry over the incident, and the next thing I knew, it was dawn—I had begun to hear sounds from the street—before I finally fell asleep.

Later that morning, crossing the row of acacias on the way to the lavatory, I came across James in the middle of the garden, intently watching the comings and goings of a wren that had settled on one of the branches and was building a nest.

Hearing my footsteps, he turned away from me. I was about to say something when I saw him slowly back off, arms clasped behind him and head down.

I took umbrage at such indifference. Undoubtedly the Commander and Basílio were right.

And never again did I meet up with him. Late into the night, from my room, I would hear his footsteps and sometimes the sound of humming, but that was all.

One night, Brandt and I were walking along Botafogo Beach, when he passed by in an open carriage.

"There goes the eccentric," said the musician, tossing the tip of his cigar onto the sidewalk. We commented on that mysterious life, and I told him about the night of "dizziness," when Brandt, after listening, said quietly:

"To me, he is a suffering soul. I would love for you to see him when I play at night. The man comes to my window and stands there listening for hours and hours. Certain songs seem to bother him, although I don't know why. I would just start to play them when he walks away, muttering nervously. Other pieces seem to attract him, such as Meyer-Helmund's 'Melodie nocturne,' and I wouldn't be surprised to see him come to the cottage one night, listen, and then leave without saying a word. He genuinely adores Beethoven and Schumann. If you'd like, come to the cottage and you'll see. And what's most interesting is that Miss Fanny worships him."

"Who? Miss Fanny?"

"Yes. In fact, I'm not sure whether he comes to the garden to hear me, or if my piano is just a pretext. They talk and spend time together. I see them out there walking until quite late."

"Miss Fanny!"

"Indeed."

"Come now . . . It's not possible. Miss Fanny? I don't believe it."

"Whenever you want to see it . . ."

"Tomorrow then . . . !"

"Perfect. Come early, at 9:00."

"Alright." We said our good-nights. Brandt went off to a birthday party for some dandy. He was scheduled to play an elegy and the "March of the Mists."

It was a stifling night. In the distance, lightning flashed over the murky sea, illuminating the heavy and turbulent sky. Gusts of winds whipped up swirls of dust.

The next night, I went to the cottage at the agreed-upon hour. Brandt was waiting for me, slowly turning the pages of the score to *Parsifal*.[4]

---

4. An opera in three acts, the last composition by the German composer Richard Wagner (1813–83). It is loosely based on a thirteenth-century epic

The layout of his room was a true reflection of the musician. There was an abundance of soft, comfortable furniture: ottomans and green Moroccan divans piled high with pillows; the large, open Bechstein grand piano; and a reed organ. There was a tall jacaranda tree and a silk marquetry screen depicting a phantasmagoric riverine landscape filled with storks flying in the distance or perched on one foot, pondering the shimmering threads of water. The plush, purplish carpet drowned out the footsteps, muting all sounds.

A cachepot on an earthenware column held a slender palm whose leaves fanned gracefully out over the edge. The walls were hung with precious paintings, engravings, portraits, scowling samurai masks, and antique porcelains; an authentic panoply was arranged around a shield topped by a Spanish helmet, and radiating from it as trophies were Indigenous arrows, blowguns, cudgels, and Indian trumpets displayed around an eye-catching feathered headdress, flanked by a tucum belt fringed with coconut bells and a lustrous, long, black shock of hair, flowing like the bushy tail of a wild colt.

The shelves overflowed with music. A green curtain covered the bedroom door.

---

poem that recounts the story of the Arthurian knight Parzival and his quest for the Holy Grail.

Brandt opened one of the blinds, allowing a flower-studded jasmine branch to lean intimately into the room.

The moonlight looked like snow.

Outside, a bit further away, the trees whispered like crumpled silk, and in the air, high-pitched, piercing screams broke the silence. It was a woman in the neighborhood giggling in hysterical falsetto.

Brandt smiled and, taking a piece of music from the shelves, opened it on the piano and sat down while quietly saying:

"I will draw him in." He ran his hands over the keyboard, pausing for a moment as he looked up, as if for inspiration . . .

His fingers moved lightly, calmly, in a flurry, drawing from his soul the melodious *Pastoral* by Beethoven. The notes sang out, scattering divine poetry, opening the senses to the mystery of nature, flying as butterflies in reverie into the dreams of the night, mingling with the perfume outside in the mystical serenity of the sleeping space, under the moonlight.

My mind wandered from the reason for that enchantment, the cause of the harmonious celebration, when the pianist, leaning into the piano, and from one second to the next, glancing out into the garden, alerted me, adding more soul into the marvelous symphony: "Here he comes!"

I was seated in the armchair next to the window and clearly saw the white figure drawing nearer, one minute under the light, the next hidden by the shadow of the languid branches.

I sat up in the armchair to see better, but to no avail; I went closer to the window and looked out: there he stood motionless, by a palm tree, listening.

Farther away, another white figure, light as the morning mist, appeared to sway at the end of the row of acacias, rocking slowly back and forth. It was Miss Fanny. And so they remained as the music played on.

Once the piano went silent, James left his spot and walked leisurely toward the teacher. They moved as pale visions, swallowed up by the shadows, flanking the arbors as moonlight drenched the garden.

"You're right. It's a romantic interlude."

"Are you convinced now?"

"It's true."

"You can see that the Englishman is not as eccentric as he seems."

"More than he seems, Brandt. Handsome as he is, with the fortune he has, he could set his sights higher and give his eyes the charms of a divine face. Miss Fanny . . . you must agree . . . A fine girl, without a doubt, but . . .

"Who knows? Miss Fanny is intelligent; her hair transforms her, and love does not need much to be happy.

There are those who focus their passion on a smile, a gesture, the sound of a voice, ignoring everything else. Sometimes, one loves the pain. Who knows? Pure souls go deeper. Neither of those two is ordinary: he is eccentric, and she is idealistic. Beauty is vain. The heart does not see, it feels. Sight comes from intelligence, not from emotion; it is in one's head . . . and the head is what floats in reality. It is one's heart that plunges into the mystery and gives it rhythm. Who knows? But enough of that. On to Schumann's *Reverie*." And he began to play the prelude.

Again, they spotted the two figures in the moonlight. In slow, careful steps ahead of his companion, James came once again to stand next to the palm tree, while Miss Fanny remained where she had first appeared, motionless and white, as if of marble.

As that sensual page ended, James silently stepped back on his path to join the teacher, and the two, blurring together, disappeared in the shadow.

"How interesting!"

"What do you think?"

"I don't know."

The hour grew late, serene and pleasant, the moonlight growing ever more pearlescent, like a flower opening in the silence. The branches swayed in the fresh breeze, shaking the fertile or virgin flowers they loved, spreading fragrance or welcoming seeds. The fragrance rose in a voluptuous serenade: it was the nuptial hymn of sensual roses, the wedding poem of the jasmines and magnolias, the divine harmony of the flowers' inner petals.

Languidly, the branches drooped, and their dark shadows, moving against the sand of the path, were like watchers of love, discreetly hiding the nighttime colloquy.

Brandt, at the window, repeated his refrain:

"Who knows? It could be a purely spiritual love; that divine affinity that creates currents of attraction between distant souls, bringing a blond man from the cold of the north into the warm arms of a daughter of the sun country. People call that mysterious force destiny. Why not call it affection? Beauty is an illusion of the senses. Beautiful, truly beautiful, is only the ideal. The bride of Menippus is a symbol.[5] There is no beauty that can resist the passage of time, and what is beautiful, like the self, is eternal.

"I must tell you: there are times when I feel passionately in love, and the woman I love (let's call her Woman, which is the expression of the feminine) does not live but

5. This line refers to the story about a young man named Menippus who falls in love with a beautiful, tempting young woman soon revealed by Apollonius as an *empusa*, a kind of shape-shifting creature in Greek mythology.

exists; she is intangible, yet I feel her. I see her on a wave of sound just as one sees the smoke that emerges from the censers. She envelops me with her essence and gives me pure spiritual joy, which is ecstasy but sweeter and more fruitful than the ephemeral spasm that brings forth death. You could say she is Melody. I don't know, I call her Love. Have you ever been in love?"

"Truly? Never. I've only had fleeting impressions."

"Fleeting . . . Love is a fixed idea: it rises from the heart as emotion and becomes thought in one's mind. Who knows? Maybe that man found in Miss Fanny the complement to his being, his feminine side. They were two yearnings that searched for each other in the ideal. Don't palm trees love from a distance?"

"And have you noticed, Frederico, that James's face has not a single masculine feature?

"It's the face of a sphinx, my friend."

"Well said: a sphinx. Good night, Brandt. And thank you for the performance."

"If you enjoyed it, come again." And, at the door, he added: "I'm still hoping to drag him in here. If Orpheus was able to tame the beasts and stop the course of the rivers with his mystical lyre, I don't think it's too much to ask for me to subdue but a single soul."

"You do have the powerful art. I'll see you tomorrow."

I got as far as the fragrant and luminous veranda when the silence was broken by the sounds of tender and moving sweetness. I leaned against the railing, listening. It was the aria of Elsa, the description of a dream, the humble song of fragility strengthened by faith, along the banks of the Scaldo, between the wicked cruelty of Frederick and Ortrud, and the indifference of the Brabantians.[6] Where did it come from? What was that voice that spread such sweet gentleness into the night?

Then, a strange exclamation sent shivers down my spine:

O my soul! Where art thou, my soul . . . !

I took a quick glance around and saw the white figure of James near the arbor, his hands raised to the heavens in supplication, and at the edge of a flower bed, a devastated Miss Fanny was weeping.

---

6. This line refers to the opera *Lohengrin*, by Richard Wagner, first performed in 1850. The opera tells the story of a mysterious knight who arrives to help a noble lady in distress. He marries her but forbids her to ask his origin, a promise she later forgets, causing him to leave and never return. By not revealing his nobility, the hero is assured that he will be admired not for his status but for his qualities.

II

One morning, Alfredo, all aflutter, came to my room with a big smile, and, while still at the door, panting, announced that the Englishman was to join us for lunch downstairs.

It was he who had taken the message. Miss Barkley was in a tizzy: she had set the table with flowers, ordered tubs of plants to be brought up from the garden, and hovered around the cook, coordinating dishes, recommending seasoning for the meats and the freshness of the eggs and lettuce to suit the difficult Englishman. Two bottles of champagne were chilling in the refrigerator, and the sweat dripping off Alfredo, enough to flatten his hair, had come from running to Largo do Machado to pick up lamb chops and fruit for dessert.

"In the dining room?" I asked with interest and disbelief, and Alfredo, with a cloth and broom under his arm, asserted:

"Yes, sir. And he has been down there on the veranda with a book since early this morning."

What a shame it was not a Sunday so that everyone could enjoy the surprise. How were Basílio, Péricles, Brandt, Penalva, Crispim, and the two inseparable brothers going to feel when they heard the extraordinary news? And poor Miss Fanny! She was out babbling with the children, going from house to house, drawing landscapes and mumbling sonatinas with only him in mind, anxiously awaiting the night.

Only old Bernaz and I were to have the incomparable fortune of seeing the divine young man nibble on the lean meat, drink the wine, munch on the grapes, sip the coffee, perhaps we would even have the pleasure of listening to the sound of his voice.

I went downstairs at the first ring of the bell, struck by the kitchen servant with the fury of an alarm, and I immediately noticed major changes in the room: it had become more cheerful by the lushness of the palms, the bright colors of the still dew-kissed roses, the cerulean sparkle of the glassware and a resplendent silver vessel overflowing with flowers sitting among festive spiral trumpet shells at the center of the table.

Miss Barkley, gaunt and tense, with her lustrous hair braided tightly around her head, came and went quickly and quietly, her spectacles sparkling at attention and her nimble fingers incessantly arranging, organizing, aligning—here a napkin, there a fork; over there, a flower.

Atop the embroidered tablecloth were woven napkins of silk and gold in festive opulence. Bottles were lined up on the buffet with a crystal ice bucket and tongs at the ready.

James, on the veranda, in his usual striped flannel, sat in a wicker chair, reading a paperback.

I walked nonchalantly by him as I headed to the stairs, admiring the clarity of the blue sky and the brilliance of the palm trees in the sun, when I sensed him get up to follow me; finally, he called out politely. As I turned, I found his hand extended in greeting, and his beautiful face, with skin as smooth and fine as jasper glowing with the freshness of young blood, adorned by his smile, was captivating.

Our handshake was truly cordial. We stared at each other without saying a word: he blushed, I felt myself pale, and as surprise stopped me on the landing of the stairs, he bowed genially and, with a gracious nod, invited me to take the first step down.

Together, like close friends, we walked through the garden where the waterfall (another nicety of Miss Barkley) gushed with abundance.

The gardener, who was trimming the grass around the flower beds, swaying to the rhythm of the scythe, suddenly stopped in astonishment and, humbly removing his hat, stood agape, with his cigarette hanging from the corner of his mouth.

Nor did I miss the bald head of the Commander, shining through the open window, following along in amazed curiosity as we slowly made our way through the manicured rose bushes.

Cicadas sang joyfully; butterflies fluttered, alighting on quivering stems; and the sun, sparkling on the sand, languidly softened the foliage in the throes of a sensual fatigue.

And James, with his gentle, caressing voice, asked, "Could I translate from English a composition of his, a kind of novel . . . Would that be too much to ask?"

"Not at all." He took me by the arm, and I, increasingly astonished, trembling as if dragged by a murderer into a hidden alley, far from any help, was inwardly delighted by the proposal that brought me to the threshold of the arcane, connecting me through intelligence to that strange man, whose beauty was a mystery, greater perhaps than his eccentricities.

"I have the manuscript. The handwriting is a bit haphazard and not always clear, but since we have adjacent rooms, any question, right? . . . I don't care how much it costs."

"Costs? What do you mean, costs?"

"Naturally. It's difficult work. Very difficult."

"That's entirely unnecessary. I don't usually translate. I've never translated, so if I make an exception, it is out of friendship, no other reason."

"Oh! No . . . no . . . ! It's difficult work. Very difficult."

"All the better, I'll benefit by improving my English."

"Oh . . . my English . . ."

"So, it is a novel?" He paused, transfigured, his mouth half open, gazing at me with his big, sad eyes, and after a moment, in a vague, elusive tone, as if confessing his love, he said:

"It's . . . my . . . novel."

A chill ran down my spine. In a muffled and trembling voice, I said:

"It must be beautiful!"

He blushed, shrugged his shoulders, pursed his lips, and, as if short of breath, anxiously shook his head, which looked like gold in the sun.

"Then I'm at your service!"

"When would you like to begin?"

"Whenever you would like."

"Tomorrow . . . ?"

"Yes, tomorrow."

"It's very difficult!" he repeated, abashed. "Very difficult." The third chime of the bell brought us back to attention. Miss Barkley, looking out over the veranda, searched the garden and, when she saw us approaching, was surprised:

"Oh! I didn't know you knew each other."

"Yes Miss . . . of course, one night . . ."

Old Bernaz, dressed in his frock coat, wrinkled his face in a grimace at the stinging of his calluses, and I could not miss the look of hatred he shot me, as if to a traitor, upon seeing me with the Englishman. James gave him a bow, receiving an irritable mutter in response. We sat down at the ladened table.

James, in his bungled Portuguese, lavishly praised the flowers and graciously offered roses to Miss Barkley, who attached them to her bodice; I stuck mine through my buttonhole. The Commander left his rose, an impressive Vermerol, on the table. James chose a Paul Neyron for himself.

Lunch was a lively affair. Miss Barkley chattered enthusiastically. The servant poured the champagne, but when offering the bottle to the Commander, the implacable man placed his palm over the top of his glass, refusing.

"You don't drink?" asked James. And the old man, without raising his head, snarled:

"Water," and asked for the pitcher. By the time coffee was served, he had loosened up, speaking a grating and broken French as he talked about the dazzling beauty of the day, the cicadas, the heat, and, on the subject of tasteless grapes, reminisced about his abundant Douro.

"Now those are grapes!"

James wanted to know why the best Portuguese wines age in the vast wine cellars of London.

"Oh yes . . . Port . . ."

"Port and others, the good ones. Portugal ends up with the dregs."

We left the table at two in the afternoon, quite mellow, and as James strolled out to the veranda with Miss Barkley, the Commander tiptoed over to me and, crossing his arms while puffing out his belly, asked through his moist pouty lips and beady eyes:

"What do you have to say about this? Explain it to me . . ."

"The man has become more human, Commander."

"He's joined us in the trenches, didn't I tell you?" And grabbing my arm, he whispered, "And he really is nice. I just noticed today. He has a woman's face, you're right. The face of a pretty woman! If Miss Fanny were to catch that one, eh? She'd give the devil a leg up." And he gave a derisive chuckle.

Despite the extraordinary activity of Miss Barkley that had lightened the servants' workload, the evening meal that day was not served until seven o'clock, under the unusual glow of all the gas lamps.

In the dining room, to which the fully extended and richly set table imparted a solemn note, between the luminous glow of the buffet mirrors and the cutlery, there was a rustle of blackberry bushes from time to time as puffs of breeze swayed the leaves of the areca and latania palms.

The guests, having heard about the great lunch event, were abuzz in whispers as they walked along the veranda.

Décio, making his customary exuberant arrival, with an appetite for art, appealing to the "brilliant" Frederico, evoker of Thracian melodies, remarked that James, the British Apollo, must have wearied of the tiresome Olympus and its insipid ambrosia, to have descended to fraternize with the mortals, coming to the table with human appetite to savor the beef stew and salad.

A heartbroken Péricles bemoaned the fact that he was caught completely unawares, otherwise he would have immortalized James's attendance by capturing it in a photograph.

"And if we were to sing 'God Save the King'?" suggested Décio. But Penalva cut in.

"Don't make fun of the man. That's terrible."

"Who?" asked Basílio scornfully.

"Who? James Marian. Do you know Felix Alvear? He's a giant."

Everyone agreed.

"A monster!" added a wide-eyed Décio.

"Well, on Sunday, after the Fluminense game,[7] just because Felix mentioned that he would like to kiss him, calling him Miss, James shoved him on the chest and, because the other tried to get him back, threw him over a fence and bloodied his face. Knocked the guy out."

"Sissies!" scoffed Basílio. "No one understands. It doesn't have to end by brute force. Either you pants the chap or give him an uppercut to the face. It's quick. That'll teach him not to mess with me!"

"And you?" Décio gestured in capoeira-esque fashion.

"I understand, I understand a little: I can hold my own. I always acted like a man! Nowadays, I'm tired . . . but even so, it's not just anyone who can take me on."

When Crispim appeared, very shy, with an embarrassed giggle, buttoning up his alpaca jacket, Basílio murmured:

"Here comes the string bean!"

They all snickered as they dispersed, and the student, exceedingly thin and freckled, his pince-nez set on the tip of his nose, his hair shaggy, passed by in silence, rubbing his hands together. And pausing among the guests, he approached Carlos, speaking softly in a near whisper about

---

7. The Fluminense Football Club, known simply as "Fluminense," is a Brazilian sports club best known for its professional soccer team, the oldest in Rio de Janeiro, founded in the Laranjeiras neighborhood in 1902.

the beauty of the sunset and the fragrance that rose from the garden when a jet of water rustled the plants.

The Commander, wearing his coat, came to the door and bowed as he waved to the group.

"Good evening, Commander."

"A little hot, no?"

"Terrible!"

But Miss Fanny, coming up from the garden, dressed in white with an orchid pinned to her bodice, put a stop to the whispering. They opened a path for her, and she quickly passed by, blushing and appreciative.

The third dinner bell chimed, and Miss Barkley appeared, drawn, gazing at everyone, and saying warmly, "Shall we?" But they hesitated.

"And Mister James?" asked the Commander.

Miss Barkley smiled and gave a shrug. "He's indisposed." It was a disappointment.

Basílio whispered, "He's drunk."

They filed silently into the dining room and sat down, and no sooner did the servant begin ladling the soup when Miss Fanny, nodding to each, stood up, covering her mouth with her handkerchief. The bookkeeper looked at her askance and, as she disappeared into the hall, snarled at Décio:

"Consumptive, my friend. She's finished. This year, she'll sing Christmas carols from the grave. Terrible voice! Also . . . one less pretty face." By the time the fish was served, the teacher had reappeared, paler and without the orchid. She sat down timidly. Every now and then she would take deep anxious breaths, raising her handkerchief to her mouth.

And the mood at the dinner table went cold. There was nothing but the clanking of cutlery to break the heavy silence. No one dared broach a subject; talk was in whispers, in hushed secrecy, between two. Sometimes, a smile would spread around the table. Even Basílio, always sneering sarcastically, devoured his meal in silence, with just a slap of his gluttonous jaws.

Suddenly Décio sprung up, kicking his chair away, his arms outstretched in a stance of adoration and rapture. In mute amazement, everyone stared at him in wonder.

The moonlight had gently descended, covering the trees in a silver haze, spreading across the veranda, and pouring into the living room. One of the palm trees in the doorway gleamed, and Décio fixed his unflinching gaze upon it as he acclaimed in rapture:

"O Rabbetna . . . Baalet! . . . Tanith! . . . Anaitis! . . . Astarte! Derceto! Astoreth! Mylitta! Athara! Elissa! Tiratha! By the hidden symbols, by the resounding sistra, by the furrows of the earth, by the eternal silence and by the eternal fruitfulness, mistress of the gloomy sea and of azure shores, oh Queen of the watery world, all hail."[8] And for a moment longer, he remained contemplative. Finally, he sat down and, serving himself a slice of roast, exclaimed:

"Magnificent!"

Everyone laughed. Miss Barkley nodded her head indulgently.

"Is that yours?" asked Penalva.

"Mine?!" Décio's bright eyes, locked on those of the young man, flashed. "How barbaric! Can't you feel the genius? It's by the divine Flaubert. The invocation of Salammbô." And, turning to the still white night, whose gentle warmth carried the fragrant touch of magnolia, he raised his glass as he extended his arm, exclaiming: "Ice, please!"

"What a memory!" crowed the Commander.

"Extraordinary!" agreed Penalva. "He can recite pages and pages. Verses, well . . . he knows entire volumes by heart. Baudelaire, for example . . . you just have to ask."

"Not quite, my friend," the student protested modestly. "I know a few poems." But then, excited, he said, "Anyone who doesn't memorize Baudelaire has no feeling, no soul."

---

8. Décio's utterance is from chapter 3 of *Salammbô*, a historical novel by Gustave Flaubert (1821–80) published in 1862.

"Pardon me, my friend," interrupted the Commander, gesturing. "I'm one of God's creatures, just like you, I mean, I have a soul, which proves I'm a Christian and I tell you this: when it comes to memory, I'm like a stone."

Basílio gave a cruel smile and, rolling his bread into a ball, asked without looking up, "And numbers, Commander? Figures . . . ?"

"Well, that comes through practice. But at school . . . History, for example. I was never good at it. I'd mix up the kings and made such a mess of things. I never got beyond the Crusades."

"But you found the cruzados,"[9] continued Basílio, rubbing his thumb over the tips of his index and middle fingers. Uncontrollable laughter exploded. With a tight smile, the Commander folded his napkin and swallowed a reply that was lost. Miss Fanny turned to Décio, lightly brushing aside the roses in a vase that partially concealed his face.

"And Tennyson? Do you know anything by him, sir?"

"Ah, Miss . . . unfortunately . . . ," he said, shaking his head in the negative. "All I know of English is cake."

"Oh! Tennyson . . . ," exclaimed the teacher, her eyes bright.

---

9. Name given to the series of Brazilian coins that circulated in the nineteenth century. The similarity in spelling and pronunciation in the English and the Portuguese provides a bit of a play on words.

"Tennyson!" repeated Miss Barkley in delight and, getting up, suggested coffee out on the veranda under the moonlight since it was such a splendid evening.

"Wonderful." And out they went. The conversation, though interesting and pleasant beneath the charm of the refreshing evening, did not appeal to me. They would laugh, and I, far off in thought, would imagine I would be struck by some remark and became wary, stifling my indignation. Pericles noticed my aloofness and, with a pat to my thigh, said:

"You're worried man."

"Distracted . . ."

In vain did Décio recite in his measured voice, faithful to the cadence, refining the rhymes and emphasizing the images; in vain did his spirit overflow in facetious mockery of literary language, exposing the absurdity of insipid elegance, remarking on the futile mimicry of the Indigenous, the latest fashions insistently forced through precious pounding into the innocent customs of our lives. They laughed. I just remained indifferent. I was thinking about the manuscript that had been promised me and that I thought I would find, back from the city, on my desk, so I could begin to make my way through it, seeking in the intrigue of the lines some sign that would help me solve the mystery of that indecipherable soul and, perhaps, who knows, the thoughts in that female head so insanely implanted on that male body, making one think about the sturdy jequitiba tree whose offshoots were like a rosebush.

When Brandt, rising excitedly, invited me to his cottage, I refused, claiming, "I was feeling poorly."

"Music is a salve. Remember Saul," said Penalva. And Décio added, trying to seduce me:

"And tonight we're going to listen to the 'Invocation of Eurydice.'[10] How can you resist?"

"I'm sick."

"Are you going to bed?"

"Perhaps."

"Outrageous! What a disgrace, on a night like this!"

"I feel sick."

"Then go. Hide away. And may nightmares haunt you!"

And the group descended into the garden, riotous and joyful, to the sound of Décio's voice reciting among the golden acacia trees:

Ce ne seront jámais ces beautés de vignettes.
Produits avariés, nés d'un siècle vaurien . . . [11]

---

10. Eurydice was a character in Greek mythology and the wife of Orpheus. The song referenced here is in act 1 of the opera *L'Orfeo* (*Orpheus*), by Claudio Monteverdi (1567–1643), first performed in 1607.

11. The first two lines of the poem *Fleurs du mal* (*Flowers of Evil*), by the French poet Charles Baudelaire (1821–67): "It will never be the beauties

Basílio stretched out his legs with a snort: "Now we can enjoy the evening."

Crispim and the brothers Carlos and Eduardo left, the first to his books and the other two to the stroll they took nightly along the Avenue to Botafogo. The Commander, sprawled in his chair, his hands across his belly, twiddling his thumbs. The two women whispered at the railing. A single gas lamp lit the room.

Pericles touched on politics and soon began the lamentations and dreadful omens and, in moonlit serenity as the flowers exhaled, the homeland, broken down to its foundations, was ground through the gossip mill, like sharp edges; it was disgraced, insolvent, disappearing, in ruins, in the bottomless abyss that was the gullet of the English. I said my good-nights, weary.

When I entered my room, bathed in moonlight, my heart raced with ominous foreboding. I glanced around the deserted interior. The sound of Brandt's piano could be heard softly in the distance. I struck a match and lit the gas, putting an end to the starlight, and stood motionless in front of my desk, mesmerized, oblivious to everything.

---

that vignettes show, / Those damaged products of a good-for-nothing age" ("Charles Baudelaire's *Fleurs du mal*").

What was keeping me from going to James? There was no reason for diffidence after the morning we'd spent together in almost confidential intimacy. I dared myself to go and resolutely stepped out into the corridor, heading straight for the parlor door.

It was ajar, and the large room, silent, with no other light than that of the moon, seemed funereal.

The impulse of courage that had brought me there weakened to cowardice. Even so, I hesitated against the gutless timidity that pulled me back to my empty and sad room, without those promised pages I craved, and to where the entirety of my soul's energy was mysteriously drawn.

I lightly pushed the door. It unleased a dry crack. I recoiled, feeling a shiver, but then pushed forward. The door yielded, opening into the pale room bathed in moonlight from the terrace. Puffs of air came my way and whistled down the hall. I clapped my hands, at first softly, but then more forcefully, until the house seemed to echo with thunder.

A white figure arose as an apparition. It advanced in slow, theatrical steps and stopped alongside the center table, its head lowered, its hands clasped together. Suddenly, throwing its arms violently into the air and its head back before shaking it in a desperate gesture, it repeated in a hollow voice the exclamation I'd heard one night in the garden:

O my soul! Where art thou, my soul!

I recognized James. I clapped louder, and he suddenly turned around, rushing to the door. I stepped forward, and the young man, as if surprised in an undignified act, retreated and fled, cringing, to a corner, where he stood, dumbfounded and mute, his arms stretched stiffly in disgust.

I called out to him once, and then again: "Mister James! Mister James!" And finally recognizing my voice, he came toward me, beaming, arms wide open, welcoming me with an outpouring of affection. In the light, his enigmatic face was like bleached marble.

He placed his arm around my shoulder. A delicate fragrance emanated from his body, and his breath, tickling my face, was warm and pleasant smelling. He cosseted me with a lover's blandishments and led me over to the terrace, where we sat down among the plants in the open air.

Again he took my hands—his were freezing—and stared at me closely with his piercing eyes, as if trying to extort a secret. But sweetly his face broke into a smile . . . a smile . . . why shouldn't I give you my impression? A smile of someone in love. And at that moment, I was certain, I was painfully, distressingly certain that the soul of that man who radiated beauty was . . . what can I say?

I mentioned the novel. He stood up suddenly, startled, then quickly walked through the room, turning on the gas, all the chandelier burners, before disappearing into his bedroom, the entrance to which was concealed by a heavy silk curtain, pearly in color, like those on the other doors that opened out onto the terrace.

He was gone long enough for me to examine the richly and tastefully furnished, yet extravagant, room.

A Louis XV grouping in yellow brocade placed in one corner was provided privacy by a folding screen brightly painted in lilacs. In the opposite corner, it was pure oriental luxuriousness: set upon a Carmanian carpet were soft cushions, concave stools, and ottomans that invited sumptuous lounging. Two large ebony chairs, carved in flowers and lace, their backs resembling the open tail of a peacock, whose plumage was depicted using exquisite inlaid shells, offered delightfully padded seats in bloodred damask and footstools that yielded to the slightest pressure, cradling one's feet in velvet softness. And on a satin-cushioned sofa, covered with gold tapestry, were magazines scattered about, some tossed randomly on the white bearskin rug stretched out underfoot.

Two porcelain vessels atop tripods exuded an aromatic substance.

And naked and graceful on a column of onyx stood a lithe and smiling marble dancer with half-closed eyes, her chest straight and stiff, her arms curved over her head, playing a sistrum, her tiny foot slightly lifted as if rehearsing the light step of a sensual ballet.

There were two tall, gilded consoles with wide-framed trumeau mirrors on which curly-headed cherubs smiled between the stylized leaves, and in the center, under the bronze chandelier, an antique table stood on spindled pillars, around which magnificent overstuffed wine-colored Moroccan leather armchairs opened their splendidly soft laps.

There was a profusion of flowers. They were in vases, forgotten alongside chairs and dying atop the consoles. Trampled on the floor were wilted bouquets of dried roses, supple as cloth.

On the table, a bulky and thick leather-bound volume attracted my intense curiosity. I opened it.

The old, grimy parchment pages crackled and cried like tin leaves. On the frontispiece were two lilies attached to a single stem—one upright, in a star-shaped bellflower, the other hanging, withered and limp. Above them was an arrow-pierced heart, dripping with blood.

I turned the page, and the text appeared in bizarre arabesques, irregular in shape and complicated in pattern: discs and sigmoids, cuneiform rods crossing or flanking Greek letters, semicircles bent over wobbly lines that among Egyptians were the symbols for water, dots, slivers, quotation marks, and scrolls. Here and there were truncated profiles of people, animals, objects—a complex ideogram; a vast, arcane enigma; or a morbid fantasy.

I was still leafing through the mysterious volume when James appeared, clutching a leather portfolio. Surprising me in the middle of my examination, he rushed forward, trembling, and in a quivering voice, flattening his hand over the open page, asked me:

"Do you understand it? Do you recognize it . . . ?"

"No. What is it?" I asked, hoping for an explanation. James fell silent, his eyes fixed on the book. Finally, he said dejectedly:

"No one knows! In vain I have explored every climate on this vast earth. For six years, in the hope of resolving these puzzles, I've traversed places where the science of the gods still exists in deep spirits. I've visited the dark temples that the earth has begun to devour. I've made my way into the woods where the yogis and sadhus,[12] paralyzed in ecstasy with parasites blooming on their shriveled shoulders, lie as if rooted to the ground, with wild grass growing all around and vipers in the deep foliage. I've climbed steep paths on rugged mountainsides on which for centuries mahatmas[13] crossed unconscious, in

---

12. *Sadhu* usually refers to a Hindu mendicant ascetic.

13. *Mahatma* is an adaptation of the Sanskrit word *mahātman*, or "great-souled." The word can refer to any person regarded with reverence, love, or respect.

an existence where time has no meaning. In caves, I've spoken to recluses older than the forests . . . and all sent me off with no hope. In Europe, this volume has been scrutinized by the renowned scholars Rawlinson, Ebers, Oppert, Maspero, Erman, and others, so many others! Some would smile, thinking me a fool, while others rejected me, affronted, as they thought me a phony. I've spent thousands of pounds . . . In vain! I would give everything I had; I'd give a drop of my own blood for each word anyone was able to pluck from these symbols that have tortured me so."

"And where did you find this book?"

"Where? At my side, in life."

"Who wrote it?"

"Arhat." In uttering that name, he shuddered as if by a shock and tossed the portfolio on the table, turning to walk away impatiently, quite agitated. He exhaled, "No one knows!" Then, calming down, he smiled, though sadness overshadowed the smile, saying with acquiescence, "And who knows the story of one's soul? Who? Everyone has a book like this, visible or invisible, don't you think? That's how life is: It's right in front of our eyes and yet we cannot decipher it . . . and it devours us. It's the Sphinx. Turn a page of this book forward—it is tomorrow, the mystery of life. Leaf it backward, and still mystery! The past, death. What is the present? It swings between longing and hope. That's how it is. What's the use of knowing? Close the book . . . or leave it open. Asleep or awake, life is always undecipherable.

"But close it. It is like an abyss, so deep you cannot see the bottom. It makes your head spin. Close it! It's a beautiful night." And he walked toward the terrace. I asked him about the novel.

"It's in that case over there. You can take it. It just needs an ending."

"You haven't finished it?" He turned pale, and suddenly, since he was within reach of the chandelier, he turned off the burners. And the moonlight again spread its spiritual clarity around the room.

Grabbing me by the arm, he pressed in closer, casting a puzzled look around. I felt him gasping for breath and the racing of his heart.

The tall palm trees out on the street sparkled, shaking their leaves in a soft and sighing movement; people and sometimes cars passed by. The sound of the piano could be heard from afar, at first faintly, then perfectly clear. James listened. Suddenly, in a departure from his thoughtful pace, he began to take long strides and repeated, "The end . . . ! I'll have it ready soon. I've hesitated quite a bit, but I need to finish it. Maybe today. The night is beautiful." And he turned his eyes skyward. "Maybe today!" He leaned over the railing, pointing to a white figure near the arbor. I recognized the young teacher.

"Miss Fanny." He shook his head and, with an enigmatic smile, murmured: "Captive . . ."

"Who?" He simply pointed to the young Englishwoman. For a moment he was quiet, but then he began to speak slowly, as if the words themselves mentally exhausted him, and, in a melancholic rhythm, he mused:

"Imagine a lioness taken to the desert in a cage and that only the slightest brush of her body would allow her to break the iron bars. Would she try to flee back to her den, attracted by the resinous scent of the forest and the roar of the heroic lions?"

"Of course."

"No."

"What do you mean?"

"She would do just the opposite: she would fortify the cage with her own body, close her eyes so as not to see the desert, make herself deaf to the seductive voices, and let herself die by holding her breath so as not to smell the musky and pungent scent of the forests. She would do this . . . if she was virtuous."

Miss Fanny walked out of the arbor. She paused for a moment in thought, picked a flower, and made her way slowly in the direction of the row of acacia trees. James murmured, "Poor lioness!"

Noting my astonishment, however, he explained, without turning around, still leaning over the ledge, and with the same slow voice:

"Arhat used symbols to express the mystery. What cannot be said or represented is portrayed through symbols. Color is a symbol for the eyes, sound is a symbol for the ears, aroma is a symbol for smell, resistance is a symbol for touch. Life itself is a symbol. Who knows what truth is? The key to the symbols would open the golden door to science, the true and only science, which is the knowledge of causes."

He spoke not to me but to the night, issuing forth the words as if slowly tossing petals into the air.

Even though deep down I was becoming more and more convinced that I was speaking to a madman, I was interested in his extravagant discourse, which took me away from the ordinary into the wild fantasy of the depraved—a dark, bristling forest, drowning here and there in bright clearings, where the chosen ones chop and clear the dream trees they use to make the lyres of poetry, the idols and the altars of religions.

"Are you from London?"

"From London?" he shrugged his shoulders. "I don't know. I grew up near London. They never told me where I was born."

"And your parents?"

"I don't know. I've never seen them. Mother . . . what a sweet word! I got accustomed to carrying it in my mouth like something that quenched my thirst for love. I lived off the perfume of an unknown flower, do you understand?" He sat down, crestfallen, bent over with his hands hanging between his knees, and went on: "You come straight to my heart, like a talisman of kindness. You just may be able to penetrate it."

"And don't you trust me? Believe . . ." He cut me off with a gesture.

"If I didn't trust you, I wouldn't have welcomed you in. And do you know why I trust you? Because you are determined, and you dream. There are two kinds of men who live alone: narcissists and thinkers. The first withdraws like an octopus—summoning all the good to himself. The second isolates himself to contemplate. One locks himself in the shadows, while the other seeks his reflection: it is as if one sits on the edge of a lake, seeing the earth, the sky, and oneself in the water. The isolated are generally naive and good: since they do not propagate confidence, they harvest no disillusions. What do you do? You live with yourself, and that is enough. One who gives himself completely to the world forgets his own self.

"I've known men and have found in them tigers, dogs, foxes, and vipers: the ruthless, the flatterer, the cheater, and the ingrate. You are one of those who hear in the silence and see in the darkness. Do you think I haven't seen you at the window late at night? What do you do? You dream. Dreaming is fecundity, it's like pollen—it takes flight but is not lost. It is not possible that the seeds of anthers have more vital energy than thought, and seeds fly through space, intersect in the open air, and fertilize. You also speak English and can understand me. Besides the women, you are the only one I can communicate with. Do you remember the first time we met?"

"Yes, I remember."

"I had just had an episode and was coming out of an aura, and you were there with me and comforted me. I owe you this kindness. The others . . ."

"You're mistaken, Mister James. If others do not seek you out, it's because they see you as withdrawn. Everyone here holds you in high regard . . ."

"Me? They hold me in high regard . . . ? Why? What have I done for them? They're curious about me, you mean. They want to study me, see what's in my soul. I've always avoided friendships so I would not suffer. If I found a true friend, I would lose them and become a wretch; if one betrayed me . . . I don't know. I had a protector—Arhat. I lived in his company, and he watched over me. It wasn't love that he surrounded me with, but care. I was his creation, a work of his genius. He took great care of me, was always attentive to my health, to my sadness, giving me medicine, defending me from every evil so I would survive. To him, I was like a delicate object kept in a display case. There was no love. What did he do for me? He gave me life, he educated me and made me heir to the fortune I'm now squandering. I was sleeping, and he woke me up . . . and now I go around tired, wishing only to go back to sleep. Give me your hand."

I did so, and he lifted it to his neck and turned it toward his shoulders so my fingers could feel his soft, cold skin. He paused at a furrow, and, following it, I could feel the outline of a wide suture, like the eruption of hives.

"Can you feel it?" He held my hand, pressing it.

"Yes."

"What do you think it is?" I hesitated before responding, and he went on to say, "It's a vestige of decapitation, right?"

I winced at this tragic statement.

"It's the necklace of death, the neck-chain that fastened me to life. Feel it! Feel it!" And, tipping his head, he guided my hand around his neck, pressing down on it, and I was able to feel a kind of erythema, in erosions and bumps, giving me a frantic shiver of repugnance.

Suddenly, throwing off my hand, he stood up.

Howling laughter roared from the garden, followed quickly by the voice of Décio:

"Excellent!" And the student appeared, stopping in front of the arbor, blowing a kiss to the night and, enchanted, declaimed to the moon in the suggestive verses of Raimundo Correia:[14]

Star of madmen, sun of insanity,
Wander, nocturnal apparition
How many drink of your splendor,
How many, sun of insanity,
Lunatic moon, there are madmen about!

"I'm leaving!" said James abruptly.

"Now?"

"Yes. You can take the portfolio and the volume. Good night!" And, putting his hand on my shoulder, he pushed me gently. I took the thick volume and portfolio and left.

14. Raimundo Correia (1859–1911) was a Brazilian Parnassian poet, judge, and magistrate. Along with Alberto de Oliveira and Olavo Bilac, he was a member of the so-called Parnassian Triad. He founded and occupied the fifth chair of the Brazilian Academy of Letters from 1897 until his death.

"Good night!" He didn't respond. The house was asleep.

I lit the gas in my sitting room and, smiling at the memory of the imperious and brusque farewell, sat down at my desk, unfastening the straps that secured the leather portfolio. It was filled with sheets of the finest-quality English writing paper.

Right from the start, I got the impression of a disturbed mind—ink spatters, erasures of lines rendering whole paragraphs useless. In some sections it was written in small, thin letters, straight and upright on the page, while in other sections there were huge and confusing characters, sometimes over smudges and drips, suspended like grass in the wind.

III

That same night I read or, rather, disentangled the entire first chapter of the "novel," with dogged patience for work more arduous than that of the diggers of ruins, who sift through the hard, bituminous, stone-filled soil of dead cities in search of antiquities.

Aside from the great deal of time it took to interpret the scrawls, to slowly and painstakingly unravel the tangled seams in scribbled plots, the successive notes were so numerous that the entire page, cross-linked with sinuous strokes broken into zigzags between the irregular lines of writing, was an intricate web, and my eyes burned with fatigue as I followed those strokes that extended to the margins, attaching themselves to their favorite word or phrase like the spool from where one begins to unwind a thread.

And, creating even more confusion, sometimes the letters curled into spirals or were wrapped in such frill that they lost their morphological character altogether, forcing me to guess at them.

Little drawings and linear landscapes interposed themselves on words like childish distractions. Sentences were finished off with symbols in the form of riddles, and often, large inkblots drowned words, truncating phrases and opening actual holes in the sentences.

Even so, I kept at it, but not without getting up many times, overwhelmed and truly amazed by what I was painstakingly extracting from that jumble of ideas.

The breeze was cooling down, and a gentle brightness began to wash over the space, showing the trees that had cast shadows. The happy cicadas sang their festive lyric poetry in chorus.

Flights of birds and butterflies announced the dawn, and the sun, still cold, threw out its first streaks of purple. The gas had almost faded away! I put it out.

I leaned out the window. The gardener, seated at the edge of a flower bed, unthreaded twine for plants, and the bustling street was awakened by the rumble of vehicles. Bells tinkled, horns sounded, and the restless leaves of the tall palms flashed golden in the sun.

Downstairs, Alfredo, barefoot with rolled up sleeves, tossed buckets of water onto the veranda, and Basílio, at the window of his room, his hair unkempt, cleared his throat of phlegm.

A pleasant fragrance rose from the garden, and the ground, damp from watering, exuded freshness.

My eyes were burning, and my whole body was bent as if in a feverish stupor. The echo of a ladle rang in my ears. I grabbed my jupon[15] and went down to refresh myself with a cold bath. My coffee with milk tasted off. I threw myself onto the bed, prostrate, but was unable to fall asleep. Outside, the hustle and bustle of life increased as the day brightened under the already warm sunshine.

I let myself remain outstretched, enjoying the sheets in a sweet lazy slumber, mentally summarizing what I had read, the strange content of those tangled pages. Finally, fatigue got the best of me, and I fell into a deep sleep as if sedated.

I awoke to the ringing of the lunch bell. I slowly dressed and went downstairs. Miss Barkley noticed the paleness of my face. I told her I'd had a sleepless night.

"Me too," snarled the Commander, sucking on his chop. "I don't know what got into the Englishman last night. He was pacing until late. I thought the ceiling was about to collapse."

"Mister James?"

"Or the devil. Evil neighbor! And look, Miss. Have the gas in my room checked because there seems to be a leak.

---

15. A *jupon* is a late medieval jacket similar to an outer coat or cloak. In this context, it describes a man's short robe.

Last night it reeked. It must be a big leak. No pipe can resist that man's jumping around. One day, the chandelier is going to fall on my head."

"He left very early this morning," said Miss Barkley.

"Who?"

"Mister James. He didn't come down to bathe."

"Perhaps he's sleeping."

"No, he's not. Alfredo came back with his coffee."

"He's around somewhere."

"In Tijuca certainly."

"Does he have relatives there?"

"Mister Smith."

"That must be it then."

I went back to my quarters, which Alfredo had straightened up and freshened with flowers, and without wasting a second to rest, I ran to the shutters to ease the glare before sitting down at my desk to open the green portfolio. I took two notebooks, numbered the pages, and, in the stillness of the house that seemed to snooze in an afternoon nap, I began to translate the strange manuscript.

The gloomy, grimy house, whose thick walls were pockmarked with scars that, like bones of a body, exposed the stones, green with slime, perennially dripping with a wet sweat, rose imposingly among the colossal trees of a park, whose background disappeared before my eyes in the dense dark branches of a forest where tall, long-lashed deer roared and skittish flocks of wild ducks answered back with rough squawks.

From my room's grated arched window that faced the sunset, where I was happy to be entertained for hours on end, I contemplated the velvety landscape and soft sky, following the gentle undulations of the hills on whose slopes small white animals frolicked. Between the hills, there was a narrow stretch of what seemed to be a frozen river, despite the sun that made it sparkle with the intense brightness of a summer day, and, rising up sleekly, sharpened into an arrow that launched itself out of a chestnut grove, was the solitary tower of a church, around which every evening at the golden hour of sunset, there would be a gulp of swallows, or, in winter, abandoned and stiff against the gray-sky backdrop, it all seemed like snow, shivering in the howling wind.

I saw not a single living soul; and voices came only from far-off animals or the croaking of my governess, a thin woman, so tall and slim that she bent like a supple, copper-colored reed, wisps of black hair escaping from beneath her silken hood. She never let me out of her sight: during the day she was always within steps of me, and at night she stretched out on a tiger skin beside my bed, on alert and on her feet at the slightest movement I made.

If I left my room, hurrying down the carpeted corridor. I was sure that her tiny black eyes, sharper than stilettos, were spying on me, following me through a crack in the doorway, and just as I would reach the spiral iron staircase leading to the top floor where Arhat lived, the woman, whose name was Dorka, would run to stop me, hideous in her striped silk clothes that gave her the repulsive appearance of a serpent poised to strike.

Sometimes, angry, in a fury, grinding her sharp teeth, she would keep me in my room, not in chains but by the power of her magnetic eyes alone that would hold me, sapping me of all energy and consciousness itself.

Only in the mornings and late afternoons would she allow me to sit by the window, gazing sadly at the cloudy distances of the unknown lands that my heart anxiously desired.

She would wake me early, at the sun's first light, accompanying me to the bath, helping me dress and then having breakfast with me.

Not even when it was time for my lessons did she abandon me. Curled up in a corner cross-legged, she never took her beady eyes off me, while my teachers (all dark-complexioned and bald) would explain the various sciences, giving me exercises in several languages, guiding me in drawing, introducing me to music, or training me in the handling of weapons.

Once a week I would go up to the great golden hall where Arhat awaited me, always melancholy and surrounded by flowers.

He was a scrawny man of average height, sallow, emaciated, and almost a skeleton, but such was the authority in his eyes as you contemplated his face that I always spoke to him in a trembling voice, even though he welcomed me with tenderness, caressing me, even soothing my tortured soul from the nightmare of Dorka, who remained just outside the door.

The golden hall, vast and magnificent, gave me the impression of bright sunshine. The walls, the columns, the majestic chandelier, and the furniture glowed as if made of light. Yellow carpets covered the floor like fine luminous grass, and the blue ceiling was truly a summer sky, from where mysterious rays seemed to descend in a shimmering brilliance that dazzled me.

The air was pure fragrance, and flowers of incomparable beauty were everywhere, in marvelous abundance.

Arhat would welcome me at the door, and before embracing me, he would stare at me with his bloodshot eyes, taking my pulse and listening to my chest. When the examination was over, he would lift me up in his arms, with a strength no one would suspect from so fragile a body. My day would commence deliciously with a light meal that came from somewhere I could never determine, appearing on the massive black lacquer table covered by a cloth whose embroidery work in a metallic luster was so elaborate that its birds and flowers seemed to have simply landed on it rather than been worked into the straw-colored fabric.

The tableware, engraved in arabesques and edged with delicate filigree, weighed down even the sturdiest of wrists. The offerings were carefully selected yet simple: slivers of cold game nestled in diaphanous jellies, vegetables, eggs, fruit on the stem among fresh greens, shaved ice, and clear water served from frosty cold vessels.

There was honeycomb on plates made of precious metal, fragrant cakes, dissolving pastilles, and an amber liquor that left a taste of violets on my tongue and put the vital heat of the sun into my veins.

Arhat would watch me eat and, in an effort to accompany me, would pick at things: a little fruit, a thread of honey, and he would smile as soon as he noticed I was full.

Suddenly, my eyelids would become heavy; the impression was instantaneous, and they would quickly open again, but by then, the table would have already disappeared. In its place would be a bronze censer, emitting a thread of blue smoke that stretched to a column or rested on an ottoman, all depending on the whim of Arhat in choosing, once again, where to reveal to me his magic, a magic to whose persistent presence I had already grown accustomed.

We would then make our way through vast deserted halls, courtyards in which stood ferocious figures—a woman with the head of an elephant, a monstrous idol from whose torso sprang numerous arms, with tiny fists holding glinting daggers; we would traverse sprawling cloisters of lacy marble arches and finally arrive at the park.

Dorka, who would wait for us downstairs, accompanied us at a distance.

Oh! The delight I felt in those carefree hours of fresh air and sunshine. I would run across the sloping lawn, sway on the swing among branches filled with bird nests, or else climb into a boat and gently row across the tranquil lake among the swans and water lilies. All of this was done under the watchful eye of the governess who would unleash guttural cries, grabbing onto the swing if I was swinging too high, calling me back to the shore if in jest I rocked the boat, or chasing me with the swiftness of a gazelle when she spied me afar, in the dense shadows of the oaks where the deer had gathered.

How old would I have been then? No more than seven.

My eagerness to experience life only intensified. At night, feeling Dorka keeping vigil at my side, I would recall the words of my teachers, all the ideas they had gradually instilled in my soul, and I would imagine the great big world that drew me to its oceans and rich and populous empires, to the intense life of its cities and the sumptuous rites of its religions. Here, green and blooming in the warm and abundant sunshine; there, barren, silent, blanketed in snow. At one extreme, thriving and well-to-do, bronzed in golden cornfields with the tranquil happiness of the harvesters' song; at the other extreme, a bloody, tumultuous war, devasting the opposing side.

And I would ask myself, "What are wars like? What are harvests like?"

And I envied the wretch who had not a straw roof to shelter him in winter, who finds not a crust of bread to deceive his hunger, not a single wool rag to cover himself and, cast out into the street, shivers and dies, more despicable than an animal.

Life, the actual path beyond those dilapidated walls, that funereal silence, those tomb-like shadows . . . how my spirit longed for it!

It was with that yearning, repressing my instincts, that I grew up sadly, and I was fourteen when the first link of the iron chain that held me gave way.

One brutal December—even though my room and the entirety of the isolated and gloomy house remained the same as it was in the mild days of spring—it was bitterly cold outside, so cold that Arhat would not even consider taking me to the park, and instead I had to make do with a few pleasant hours in the greenhouse, among the palm trees and tropical orchids.

One night in that brutal December, while I was awake, I saw Dorka suddenly sit up, gasping, her left hand slumped on her chest.

Her tousled head thrashed about, and her hideous face, thinner and yellower in the lamplight, twitched in anguished fits.

A loud snore rumbled in her throat, her bones cracking in continuous shaking, straining then relaxing her bare, dried-out legs.

I was about to get up to help the poor soul but felt trapped, tethered to my bed, unable to even turn around: my body paid no attention to my will, and my eyes, opened wide in fear, saw more clearly, and my hypersensitive ears heard more distinctly.

I reacted in frustrated surges and was still struggling in vain when I saw the door open and Arhat appear, dressed in an extravagant silk kimono, followed by a giant black man with a leather breastplate and short wool skirt, whose fringes extended to his knees.

He quickly bent over and removed Dorka's limp body in his massive arms, leaving with the frightened haste of a thief in flight.

Arhat sat at the foot of my bed and began to murmur mysterious words, waving his hands in enigmatic gestures. Then he removed a charm from his waistband, took between two fingers a bit of resin, and summoned a flame, walking around the room in whispered prayer, shaking the blend of oils to disperse the purifying smoke throughout the room. Finally, he approached me, placing his hand on my forehead before leaving. And soon I was free of the grip that had held me back in agonizing inaction.

And that was the first time I was ever afraid. Death had brushed by me, and despite the dislike I had for the governess—the power of habit is so strong!—I missed her presence, her screechy voice, her beady eyes that burned like hot irons, her constant stalking, her repulsive, scrawny, crooked face.

I wandered aimlessly around the room, stunned, in a daze that caused me to stagger and fall against the furniture, but sleep surprised me. I had barely reached my bed before I fell into a deep slumber.

When I awoke the next morning at the usual time, I saw at my bedside two motionless figures that appeared to be marble, so white and rigid were they. But the blue eyes of one and the brown eyes of the other held so much life, the smiles of both were so sweet, the color of their cheeks so healthy, and the gesture with which they greeted me, their arms crossed over their chests so gracefully, left no doubt in my mind as to their nature.

The blue-eyed girl wore her blond hair in a long, loose braid interlaced with strands of turquoise, a purple, high-necked, buttoned bodice and a short silk skirt, and her slender feet were clad in slippers with upturned toes.

Gold rings hugged her toes, and her plump arms were wrapped in bracelets from which hung jangling symbols and amulets. Maya was her name.

The dark-eyed boy, an elegant and strong young man, was dressed in belted, baggy shorts, a jacket over a puffy shirt, and suede silver-buckled boots, and on his head, debonairly tilted to allow his jet-black hair to fall in a curl over his forehead, was a cap, a kind of fez, the side of which held a gold rosette securing a black feather that rippled in the air. He said his name was Siva.

What happened to me then could only be described as "vexation." My cheeks burned in self-consciousness, and no words came to my lips, so flustered was I in front of those smiling young people.

But the young man spoke, and I, who up to that point had heard only harsh voices, was blissfully surprised by the melodious sound with which he announced himself as "my servant," humbly asking for instructions as to my desires.

But then I turned to another gentle introduction—it was the young woman who repeated the words of her companion, and, to my amazement, I found myself between two beautiful smiles, under the caressing light of blue eyes that seemed to bring a spring day, and brown eyes that brought a velvet night of moonlight and dreams.

Oh, the death of Dorka! The death of Dorka! How it seemed to be a good thing . . .

Feeling ready to leave my bed, the two young people moved away, the young woman's footsteps echoing through the chamber.

Finding myself alone, even though I could feel their presence nearby, I went into the bathroom, where, as always, everything awaited me, from the water streaming out of the scowling faucets of the marble pool to the lighted scent dispensers, misting the room with fragrance. In the dressing room, all my clothes in order, I left.

Again, the silvery sound of jingling bracelets excited me, preceding the already coveted return of the blue eyes and graceful black feather that waved along the edge of the curtain.

During meals, in the oak room where the dishes came up by dumbwaiter, the two flanked me at the table as they took turns serving.

If he took a plate, she, smiling and solicitous, brought the cutlery; if he brought over the amphora of wine, she proffered the cup; if one offered me fruit from which to choose, the other brought a basket of sweets, the bracelets always jingling, and the graceful black feather always waving.

They disappeared at lesson time. But as soon as the last teacher left, they came back, always smiling.

He wielded a kind of lyre, whose name—vina—I came to learn later; she carried a branch of flowering acacia.

Since they would find me at the arched window facing the sunset each day, where I would stand, soaking up the evocative melancholy of twilight, they sat close by on a Shiraz rug, and while the dying sun bled over the hills, the voice of the young woman blended with the sound of the instrument and drew from my heart to my eyes the first tears I had ever cried.

And there the mysterious moonlight found us.

I was overcome by fatigue. The afternoon had already turned pale in the dread of impending nightfall when, drained and exhausted in the chair, I raised my arms in a huge stretch, momentarily resting before rereading the first draft of my translation.

I was not entirely unhappy, although on one or two points, given the absence of corresponding terms in the two languages, I was only able to extract the notion, abandoning the expression, and, in certain truncated sentences, due to forgetfulness or the frequent blots that blackened the text, I completed the thought as I deemed most appropriate, always keeping in mind the action and meaning of the sentence.

And I thought about what I had read about that dream life in an unnamed place, whose vague landscape, one minute under the sun, the next in the mist, could just as well be a romantic province of France, a London suburb, a quirky Berlin neighborhood, the outskirts of Moscow, or the mystical Stockholm, cerulean in the depths of winter.

Yes, it was a dream that affirmed itself over the course of the cerebral narrative, growing stranger, crazier, and more beautiful, full of images like a magical opera.

James had wanted to give me a sample of his imagination and, with subtle ingenuity, had carefully prepared the scenes in the parlor and the delivery or, rather, the abandonment of the manuscript that I was to translate, not without interest, as I would have in the fortunate event that an unpublished tale of Princess Scheherazade[16] had fallen into my hands through the influence of some benevolent genius.

After quickly freshening up, I got dressed, and, leaning out the window, silently accompanying the end-of-day goodbyes, the slow dissolution of colors, the religious

16. Scheherazade is the storyteller in the Middle Eastern collection of tales known as *The Thousand and One Nights*.

hush of noises, the ecstatic retreat with which nature intones its evening prayer, I became aware of a sound coming through the air from far away, joyously rising as a festive voice to rouse me.

Already the stars were shining.

Again, now more clearly, the sound vibrated in the silence. It was the bell from downstairs. I lit the gas and, after catching a quick glimpse of myself in the mirror, went down for dinner.

All the guests were at the table with the exception of James. No one noted his absence. Miss Fanny, with her eyes always downcast, seemed paler and sadder than usual, coughing in frequent fits. The butler served, attentive to Miss Barkley's eyes.

Pericles, with his napkin tucked into his collar, took the floor, radiant: He had developed an exquisite photographic plate he'd entitled *Réverie d'une jeune veuve.*[17] A young woman dressed in black standing by the waterfall in the Parque da Acclamação,[18] her elbow resting atop the rock, her chin between two fingers, gazing despondently.

A widow, no doubt, and beautiful . . . but her demeanor, the rippling line of her slim figure, the air of wonder! . . .

---

17. French for "Reverie of a young widow."

18. The original name of what is now called Campo Santana, located at the Praça da República in downtown Rio de Janeiro.

He thought he'd seen a tear in her eyes. And that dark, rugged background of rough stones and crisp leaves . . . A trouvaille![19]

Basílio looked at him askance, nudging the Commander, who smiled, his cheeks bulging with mashed potatoes. And Pericles, from the vegetable soup to the guava, went on and on about photography—about the great advances in the technique, about a lens he had ordered, about certain plates that had extraordinary sensitivity, about the future of photography in the world, about all the progress contained within the four black walls of a darkroom.

The bookkeeper listened in silence, devouring a plum with his toothless gums. Finally, spitting out the pit and wiping his glistening lips with a napkin, he said:

"That explains it." Everyone turned to look at him as he smiled.

"What?" asked Pericles, stiffening with suspicion.

"What you ask? The reason why there's so little water in the Santana waterfall. It's because the widows go there to cry."

"Well!" muttered Pericles, with a dismissive gesture. And thus ended the evening's entertainment.

19. A French word meaning "lucky find."

Leaving the table, Brandt took me by the arm and, drawing me over to the veranda, asked mysteriously:

"Did you see Miss Fanny? Did you notice?"

"Miss Fanny? What about her?"

"You didn't see her crying?"

"Miss Fanny?"

"Yes."

"Don't tell me."

"I give you my word! There were tears flowing. What could that mean?"

"You're asking me?"

"Is it because of him?" I shrugged my shoulders. And the maestro voiced his pity with a smile. "The poor thing!"

Pericles, ranting in a group, gesticulated wildly as he raged against the Commander and Basílio, who were assailing the cinematograph as "a magic lantern with delirium tremens."[20]

"And the phonograph? The cinematograph is life in action, and what about the phonograph and all its noisy mechanics that whine and roar, terrifying the city? . . . Ah! Why have you nothing against that ignominy? The future of photography, my friends, is assured. Everything will go out of style: books, newspapers, even letters, you

---

20. *Delirium tremens* is a violent delirium with tremors caused by withdrawal from alcohol after excessive, prolonged use.

know? Even speeches. Every document will be photographed: a signature can be forged, but a person cannot. And politicians, instead of wasting words in tedious speeches no one reads or listens to, will transmit their ideas through photography, showing there, on the screen, the advantages of their projects, expounding their plans live, not deluding gullible people through clever verbiage."

"And instead of saying, 'what a great orator,' they will say 'what a photograph!'" teased Basílio, as he burst into derisive laughter.

"And why not? Why not?" blasted Pericles, purple. "Why not? It will be the golden age, the age of silence and action. Everything will be done cinematographically.

"A thief steals our wallet, a murderer stabs us with a knife, bam! The device records not only the person, but the movements, and all you need to do at the trial is develop the film to see the monster projected on the courtroom screen, with a clear X on his back. And the phonograph?" he bent forward, with bulging eyes. "Deeds, not words, my friends. *Res non verba*, as Cicero and others would say," he concluded, using a wad of tissue to sponge the copious sweat off his face.

Crispim, picking aggressively at his teeth with a toothpick, stirring up the dilapidated tooth stumps, hooted a silly laugh, sucking in the shards.

Brandt invited me to come listen to a bit of music.

I refused. I felt like I needed to move, get some fresh air and a little tranquility.

All those hours spent in hard labor, the sleepless night, the concerns I felt over the character of that man whose life I was beginning to see into through the gold and ivory door of an extravagant dream had truly strained my soul. I went out.

Pedestrians enjoying the cool evening air strolled along the street, with its long column of palm trees like the gallery of a temple. Servants passed by, returning from their day's work.

In the shadows of the gardens, children chattered, white figures nestled in the warmth of the trees where they seemed to lie sweetly drowsing. From some of the illuminated houses came the sounds of piano.

I walked slowly toward the avenue. The palm trees rustled unceasingly. Crowded streetcars passed by in a flurry. In the threshold of a door that opened into a dark passageway, two men in shirtsleeves, their legs outstretched, sat humming a melody.

The nearly deserted broad avenue, where pearls of lamplight spread their white glow, was as silent as if asleep.

Every few minutes, an automobile would roar by, or a slow carriage would make its way along, its coachman erect and his passengers silent, dejected and sunken into their seats as if returning from a funeral.

I leaned against the seawall, gazing out over the sparkling sea.

Soft and lazy waves broke in spurts, like the measured emptying of a bucket. But the sky behind the hills gradually brightened as a harbinger of dawn, and a curved thread of light shone, lacing the tops of the ridge in snowy white, as the enormous disk that was the moon rose with the spectral impenetrability of a vision, spreading a long silver gleam over the water.

There was a fiery burst of light as a wave thundered onto the sand and then cooled.

Groups of people were beginning to approach, enthralled by the moonlight: intimate couples, babbling children, and from the direction of Botafogo, as if in a mad race, came carriages, automobiles, and bicycles, raising a cloud of dust that flowed back in waves, dimming the lights before rising and disappearing.

A man walked slowly toward me. He stopped when he reached me and slowly removed his hat, his white, stringy hair appearing damp, and his sour-looking beard dripping from his emaciated face, glistening in an oily sheen. He gazed at me, humbly bowed his head, and extended his trembling hand, mumbling a request in which I thought I heard something about family.

I gave him a coin. He bowed, humiliated, with a slight wave of his hand in gratitude, and wandered slowly away along the embankment. A few steps along, he stopped for a moment, indecisive. Finally, in the solitude of the avenue, he decided to step away, looking for shelter, people, souls who would listen to him and take pity on his wretchedness.

He looked around, fixated on something in the distance and, with a show of effort, quickened his steps and bent down further, disappearing into the shadows among piles of bricks next to construction scaffolding. He reappeared, further down, under the glare of a streetlight, and returned to the corner.

And me? Where would I go? I felt incapable of taking a single step. My legs gave way a bit, but my spirit, in avid curiosity, implored me to continue that adventure I had begun, where I was heading, with such unusual pleasure, to unveil, with every sentence, as through the branches that spread out in a forest of wonders, greater secrets and more beautiful delights.

I purposely turned toward home. As I approached, I thought I saw a figure among the trees. I extended a greeting. And the sweet voice of Miss Fanny responded from the shadow.

The magnolia gave forth an agreeable scent. Brandt played his piano. Miss Barkley and the Commander chatted as they sat in the wicker chairs on the veranda. I paused for a moment, admiring the night, when the Commander spoke to me:

"We're free of the Englishman for a while. He wrote to Miss Barkley, requesting a few things. He's in Tijuca with Smith. May he stay there as long as he can."

Miss Barkley, in a departure from her usual discretion, expressed for the first time her puzzlement over his mysterious life. It wasn't natural. Lots of people have their eccentricities, but not like him: it was too much. Anyway . . . Since he wasn't a bother . . .

"Wasn't a bother?" exclaimed the Commander. "That was the least of it. There is no worse neighbor."

"That was just one night," I said, in his defense. "Obviously you weren't tired. Our rooms share a wall, and I didn't hear a thing, even though I was awake."

"Oh sure . . ."

The sound of Brandt's piano silenced the conversation. Miss Barkley leaned against the rail in interest. It was a Liszt[21] rhapsody played with expression and ferocity.

"He plays well!" admitted the Commander.

Miss Barkley nodded her head, enraptured. "Oh! Very well!"

---

21. Franz Liszt (1811–86) was a Hungarian composer, virtuoso pianist, and teacher from the Romantic era.

And silently, we listened to the wonderful piece.

I rose, yawning, ready to head to bed, with noble ideas about my work the next day: I would rise early and, after bathing, resume the translation until lunchtime, when, after a short rest, I would keep at it until nightfall. But, in my room, in front of my desk, curiosity got the better of me. I opened the front of the desk, slowly leafing through the convoluted manuscript, then sat down, laid out paper, took up my pen, and was about to write my first word when I heard voices, an unusual commotion downstairs: hastening footsteps, slamming doors, chairs roughly pushed away. I ran to the top of the stairs to listen and was able to make out the voice of the Commander, who said in alarm:

"Is anyone there? Anyone? Avail yourself, young man!"

Bending over the railing, I asked:

"Is there something wrong, Commander?"

The old man, who was nearby, came up a few steps and, cupping his hands around his mouth, whispered breathlessly:

"Miss Fanny, the teacher . . . there's blood pouring from her mouth. It looks like it's from her lungs."

I descended to meet him on the step. Then, confidentially, he explained:

"We were on the veranda when she appeared, coughing in anguish . . . She was clinging to a column, and when we approached her, there was a spurt of blood, more than a liter, I don't know." He scratched his head, his face twisted in horror and disgust. "They sent for a doctor. How long have I been suggesting that? A weak creature like her, leading the life she leads? Someone who works without rest, day in and day out; what more could such a creature take? That's what you get from ambition. And with no family, poor thing."

"Did they give her anything?"

"I don't know! Miss Barkley is preparing some potion with wine. She's doomed . . ." I went with him further downstairs. "Don't bother. You have work to do, let it be. Good night. Let it be."

"But if it's necessary . . ."

"No, it's not." And he turned around, repeating, "Let it be, because she's already in her room, and as you know, the sun doesn't shine there . . . just the moon, because it is feminine. The doctor will be here soon. Good night."

And he disappeared down the hall. I remembered the mysterious line uttered by James: "Poor lioness!" And for a while I stood there, leaning against the banister, watching, as if expecting something else to transpire, news of another gush of blood, the last one, then death. But the house descended back into silence.

I went upstairs, making my way through the corridor when I sensed the light from the gas burner flicker, in trembling flashes. I looked up: the flame was in fact shrinking, as if a mysterious hand was slowly twisting the knob. Suddenly, the light went out.

A beam of moonlight whitened the floor, striking the wall. But the light became more concentrated, coming together into a cloud, as if there were a skylight in the corridor, filtering the night's sad paleness into a circle. And from the floor, a rising brightness grew, taking shape in the shadow.

A slender figure appeared, dressed in a voluminous tunic, the soft outlines of which enveloped a female body. White as plaster, and still as a statue, it held my eyes, and as its facial characteristics grew clearer, I recognized in them the features of James.

From the soft folds of the tunic emerged bare white arms, whose white hands stretched out toward me. It was James Marian, and in that attire, his face was even more beautiful. It was him, as I had imagined in my dream.

Terrified, unable to move from the spot where the darkness had surprised me, I stood there, frozen by a chill of dread, my mouth going dry and my heart pounding.

But the light reappeared, the gas rekindled in a blue flame, at first tiny and tentative, then growing like an unfurling flower, and the vision dissipated, dissolving into the clarity until again the corridor appeared illuminated and deserted.

Then I was able to walk although transfixed. I opened my door, but before going in, fearful of seeing yet another apparition, I stopped to examine the inside. Everything appeared in order. I breathed as if having been rescued from a disaster.

But my legs went slack, and I let myself fall back onto the divan, overwhelmed, breathing heavily, strangled by fear.

The house seemed alive, expanding and straining its stone limbs, all its timbers, teetering on its very foundation.

Great noises echoed from one piece of furniture to another, or the ceiling boards were splintering, rattling the fearful silence with loud booms.

At times, the light flickered in oscillations that altered the room's appearance, the position of the shadows moving as they shrank and then grew. And I, as if penetrated by the cold of death, felt my heart near bursting, and my blood went from flowing out to leave my head hollow, to rushing to my brain, stunning me into a state of complete apoplexy.

I stood up, taking great strides through the narrow corridor, avoiding the mirrors through inexplicable fear, but out of the corner of my eye, I caught sight of my reflection, without ever taking a full look, certain that I would find it transformed, if not in fact the image of another person.

I reached the bedroom door and pulled back the curtain—a sliver of light came through the crack to the edge of the bed, but the room's interior was black, in darkness. And in that darkness, I felt something undecipherable, an impalpable betrayal, the trap of the invisible mysterious.

I went back to the sitting room and, without even turning off the gas, grabbed my hat and left.

Still in the corridor, I hesitated before turning the key, and finally, determined, I turned and walked silently down the stairs, ashamed of the cowardice of that escape. I walked through the still-lit dining room, the veranda, the garden, and then aimlessly ventured out into the street.

I caught the first streetcar that came along, eager for the hustle and bustle of life. But the whole city was filled with my terror.

In the darkness of the solitary streets, thin, funereal silhouettes gliding through the air crossed my path, hovering before my eyes as halos before suddenly disappearing. In the groups themselves I felt and sensed the presence of some vague ethereal being that integrated itself among the living as if to take refuge.

I walked until late, wandering. I went to all the popular spots but felt the ill-omened influence of an evil force, everywhere and in everything.

In a run-down bar, tucked away in an alley, broken-down women in rowdy vagrancy, elbows perched on filthy tables, glassy-eyed and drooping from intoxication, smoked and chatted with the hustlers of the night to the twangy sounds of an accordion being played.

I stood at the door, breathing in the exhalations of the low-life camaraderie, but the depravity turned sinister, and the rakes and hussies who were huddling together seemed to me mere visions that would dissolve, like the smoke that filled up such dives. A carriage passed by with joyful voices—two boys and two girls. I took a tilbury[22] and ordered the driver to follow them, wanting to latch onto that wanton extravagance. They alighted at the Paris ballroom, and I followed them in.

The ballroom was abuzz with excitement. I wandered over to the first free table I saw, and, listless, inert, and exhausted, I surrendered myself to the will of the waiter who was serving supper. Looking at myself in the mirror, I was almost surprised to see the same me, so different did I feel inside.

I would have stayed until dawn in that hubbub, under the bright lights of the chandeliers, were it not for the night owls who started leaving in all different directions, some singing, in the company of young women, hats at the nape of their necks, flinging their legs in jerky dance steps; others slow, thoughtful, sullen, and yawning.

---

22. A light, two-wheeled carriage.

I left to plunge back into the night that had terrified me.

The moon had vanished, obscured by thick clouds. A strong wind blew.

At the door, I thought I heard Décio's voice in a group.

It was him indeed, dressed all in white denim, a tuberose in his buttonhole. He was talking about Rodenbach[23] with his usual flare and hyperbole. He saw me and came forward, his eyes sparkling:

"What's this? You? The homebody . . . at two o'clock in the morning, without an umbrella and cloak, at the entrance to the Paris club? What's this? What great changes threaten this dreadful land?" And he drew closer, patting me and checking to convince himself it was me. "But is it really you? What's going on?" he asked quietly, with a smile on his boyish face. He took my arm, saying a quick good-night to the group that soon dispersed, and dragged me into the middle of the square.

"Come on, tell me. Pour tonight's adventure into the abyss of my discretion. Tell me about the sheen of her hair, the color of her eyes, the winged grace of her walk. Is she an intellectual with a soul, or an unrefined Venus,

---

23. Rodenbach is a legendary Belgian brewery founded by the Rodenbach family in Roeselare, Belgium, and is synonymous with the Flanders or Flemish Red beer style.

an illiterate and bawdy good-for-nothing? . . ." I told him of my terror.

"What? In that house? That's impossible!"

"It's true. I don't know what it was . . ."

"Perhaps bad wine at dinner."

"I didn't drink."

"Well then, my dear man, you're a darling of the gods, the only man on this worn and weary planet given to enjoy the magnificence of a thrill. Because there are no more thrills. Baudelaire used up the few that were left. And you found one! . . . You're a lucky man! And you left that exquisite sensation to splash around in the mud of this infected underbelly! If you promise me a little of your fear, a shiver at least, I'll go with you, I'll spend the night by your side. If not, come with me to Copacabana, visit the old ocean, and enjoy a frosty beer, the dew that gives bloom to my lyricism on sentimental nights. Come on, make up your mind!"

I took him with me. He stayed on the divan in the sitting room and, until late, leafing through volumes, rattled the silence with the music of stanzas and bursts of enthusiasm.

IV

I awoke, dejected and exhausted, my entire body aching as if it were bruised, and my head heavy like an immense fog-filled space, crossed here and there by a thin thread of a memory.

I stretched out and pulled up the covers, warmly ensconced in the cradle of the bed, and looking at the ceiling, I began to think about the incident of the preceding night. As the sun began to poke through the blinds, illuminating the room, shining on the furniture and glistening in the mirrors, I realized how ridiculous was the trepidation I'd felt so strongly that it had sent me running from the house in fear in the middle of the night.

Then I remembered Décio: I called out to him with repeated insistence. I heard steps hurrying into the sitting room, and Alfredo drew back the curtain, saying, in a surprised voice:

"Mr. Décio? He left a while ago. He bathed, had a cup of coffee, and went out. Shall I bring you your coffee? I already did, but you were sleeping."

"Yes, bring it. But first: how is Miss Fanny?"

"I think she's better. But, just between us . . ." He stuck out his lip as if hopeless and, thumping his chest, said, "It's her lungs, consumption. Don't you think so, sir? I've scrubbed the veranda, scrubbed it hard, but the stain is still there. Buckets of blood. And she also spit up in her bedroom, and the gardener told me she had done so in the garden as well. After all, people don't have as much blood as wine in a vat. As you know, once gone, it never comes back, and that's life. So, coffee, yes? Do you want milk?"

"No."

"Black. Very well." He propped up his broom and ran off.

The morning was useless. After lunch, I sat down at my desk, opened the portfolio, and spent a long time just staring at the dense pages, riddled with scratches and dotted with stains that further complicated my understanding of those intricate scribbles.

I got up and went out into the corridor, wanting to see where the vision had appeared to me. I carefully examined the floor, walls, and ceiling, as if looking for some sliver through which the fluid body had emerged before me like a statue, stopping me cold. And there, I forgot about myself, my mind numb, my gaze inert, frozen in breathless contemplation of the nonexistent.

I went back into the sitting room, smiling at my terror; opened the window to the sun; lit a cigarette; and, sitting down at my desk, continued the translation:

From that day forward, my life changed like a river that, rolling in anguish through a shadowy gorge, over a bed of stone-spiked mud, emerged in relief over a verdant plain, flowing through lush trees under blue skies and the ceaseless flight of birds and butterflies.

The hours passed without my even realizing them, peacefully easy and sweet with the tender attention of my companions in solitude.

The greatest proof of the charm they knew how to create around me, ever since I had them with me, was the indifference with which I approached the day, once so highly anticipated, when Arhat would welcome me to the magnificent gold ballroom and indulgently follow me to the park, allowing me to walk freely along the silent paths, soaking myself in the light and the smells, to run on the beautiful grass, to paddle in the lake, to climb up the slopes of the grassy hillsides, to rest among the wet stones and listen to the warbling of the water, to see up close the darting grace of the does or the haughty carriage of the rugged bucks, whose multipoint antlers appeared among the chestnut trees like the roots of unearthed trees.

In all this joy, the only annoyance to disturb the sweetness of my life arose from the sudden changes, the volatility in which my indecisive and changeable soul struggled between unabridged affection for Siva and complete devotion to Maya.

Some days my heart beat frantically, demanding the young man and rejoicing in intense pleasure when I felt him nearby. Simply the whisper of his footsteps caused a happy commotion inside me, and if he spoke, I felt my blood course through my veins, my cheeks burn, and my eyes, seeking his, grow damp with a flood of tears.

If the young maiden appeared to me when my propensity was for the brown eyes, I became irritated to no end and had trouble containing the sudden impulse of resentment.

At other times, however, the same feeling would manifest itself with regard to the graceful feather so close to the shining hair. Then it was the maiden in whom I delighted.

I wanted her close to me and would take her hands in mine, clasping them passionately, trembling at the sight of her tiny, half-open mouth; her warm bosom; her slight waist; and her delicate toes clasped with gold rings.

And my pleasure was to be alone with her, silent, my eyes gazing at her face, our hands entwined, watching her work, smile, and blush as she lowered her eyelids, her breath quickening to breathlessness and her rosy cheeks growing redder.

This affection alternated between the two but always carried the same trace of hatred for what remained out of reach, as if my heart could no longer contain affection for both figures at once, and I feared losing in the one chosen the seductive features of the one shunned.

Such fickleness troubled me, and remorse punished me after the rejections. Then, to forgive myself for what I judged to be an offense, I appeased myself, attributing the frenzy that caused me to act so at odds with how I felt to nerves. The response from each was always a smile, and then they would compete, redoubling their affection, pampering me more and attending to my desires, which they divined in order to fulfill.

By the age of fifteen, I was as physically mature as I am today, time completing the man by adding a bit more robustness.

In contrast, however, my soul grew weak as my body grew strong. I felt one instinct fade as other inclinations intensified.

The dashing courage of my early years cooled to timidity; my taste for weapons, for exercises in dexterity, for daring moves waned, and the adventurous spirit that caused me to crave the world with all its dangers faded. My ideas seemed to be replaced by others.

My intelligence, once so sharp, ready, and inquisitive, shut itself down with distaste for certain studies, and instead of books, I began to prefer flowers. I exchanged weapons for tapestries and found more interest in the weaving of a gold or silk weft thread or in the melody of a love song than in the wise lessons or the gallantry of a well-bred horse on which I followed Arhat, a rider as brave and bold as a centaur.

One night—it was in the winter, and it was snowing—a cheerful fire was burning in the massive bronze and marble fireplace, spreading a bright purple glow all around. I was reading, cozy and warm, when I suddenly shivered, a harsh chill coming from behind me as if one of the tall windows had opened, causing me to feel a sharp blast of winter air hit my back.

I turned around in fright: all the doors were bolted shut, not a puff of air was coming through, so stiff were the folds of the curtains that hung motionless. It grew colder, however, even though my hands and face retained the usual warmth of that heated environment.

I drew the chair closer to the fire, but it was as if I had leaned against a block of ice. I tried to cover myself better by pulling the furs more tightly around me, but the unpleasant and morbid sensation persisted, taking over my body and causing my teeth to chatter.

I wanted to stand up and call out, but I was paralyzed, and I don't know how long I sat there wrapped in the furs, pierced with cold, watching the glow of the flame, and listening to the crackling of the firewood.

It was an internal cold, as if my blood was freezing and my bones were made of snow. Little by little, however, the warmth came back and, with it, a heavy sleep, the sleep of fatigue so extreme it laid me out as if dead.

The next morning, I awoke with such happiness and energy that Maya smiled at my glee as she came in with an armful of orchids gathered from the greenhouse.

When I saw her, laying down the sword I was using for exercise, I put my arm around her delicate bosom, kissing her twice on her forehead and mouth.

She did not seem surprised, but happy, and, giving in to my delirium, simply lowered her eyelids, and her small hands were like snow, trembling inside my own as I clutched them tightly.

What I then felt for that creature, whose name became the purpose of my lips, was true detachment of my being, a submissive surrender of my soul that seemed to have transmigrated into her body that I adored, from the golden strands of her hair to the tips of her dainty feet that brought her in contact with the ground.

I craved the very shadow she cast, since it was the extension of her body, the part in the light, so much so that once, having gathered all the flowers that scented the chamber and my room, I made her stand in the sun while I used them to cover the shadow of her body so as to trace it on the chamber's carpet. That night, instead of lying in my bed, I, like the groom who seeks out his bride, lay on the shadow and fell passionately asleep in the dream of my love.

Listening to her was my pleasure. Seeing her seated, I would kneel at her feet and get lost just gazing into her eyes, seeing myself in them as in the liquid transparency of a lake.

My greatest joy was to feel her heart, counting her heartbeats and matching them to my own. We would smile at each other, amused by such delight, and sweetly, our heads would seek each other out, our lips joined together: I breathed in the breath of her bosom, and she drew the breath from my chest, and in that exchange of breaths, we lived off the intimate atmosphere in which our souls hovered.

And so, absorbed in each other, we even forgot the time. The night would surprise me, but how could I have realized it with the luminous blue of those eyes and the astral splendor of that golden hair?

Siva, with not a single sign of contempt for the preference with which I singled out and doted on his companion, visited less and less frequently, until he limited himself to appearing just once, in the morning, standing in the doorway, motionless and silent, with eyes downcast, awaiting my instructions. He would receive them and remove himself for the rest of the day; not even the sound of his footsteps could be heard nearby.

And like that, in this sweet colloquy, a month slipped by serenely.

I had become so absorbed in Maya that it was only after a long time that I realized that four times Arhat had neglected to welcome or even communicate with me. Four weeks had passed without my seeing him, the first since my earliest childhood!

Although they had not taken away my freedom, which Arhat had granted me on the happy day he announced, with fatherly pride, that I had turned fifteen and could walk freely in the park and in all the rooms of the manor that were made available by those who served me, I felt uneasy and confined without the comforting and gentle presence of that friend.

I asked Maya to explain that oblivion that offended and hurt me like unpleasant abandonment.

She did not answer. I pressed her, cajoling. She made a gesture with her hand, pointing into space, the beyond, as if to mean he had left. And that was as much as I could gather from her discreet silence. But the next morning, I questioned Siva, and the young man, gazing at me with his soft, dark eyes, said:

"Sir, Arhat will return with the sunny days when the swallows fly. He is traveling. You will have him with you when the first birds of spring appear." That was all he said.

From that time on, inexplicably, the flame that had impassioned my heart began to cool. I had already become unattentive to Maya, I would avoid her footsteps, and surprisingly, her dear voice began to take on an annoying tone.

I spent my days absorbed in solitary reflection, and at night, awakening, I would get up, tiptoe barefoot over the carpet to the door, and open it to the vast hall lit by opaque lamps whose carved foliage looked like lilies and magnolia, and I would stare out, with an intense desire to go up the spiral staircase to the ballroom and open the small entry door to a sort of secret chamber from where Arhat often emerged. His quarters must have lain just beyond that.

But the fear that I would be caught in such profligate intrusion, and that I would potentially incur the displeasure of the all-powerful man, kept me from doing so.

Late one night, however, when the wind blew furiously and the snow was heavy—the entire house was asleep—I got up and, with determination and steadfast resolve, set off for the hall.

My footsteps cracked on the carpet like green wood in a fire, and I was shaking all over even though I had thrown a fur robe over my shoulders. I walked on and stopped in front of the stairs.

The lamps cast a dazzling light over them, the hand-rail sparkling like a silver scroll, and at the top, in the circular opening, it seemed even brighter, like sun streaming through a skylight.

Fearfully, I began to climb; my knees buckled, so extreme was the trembling.

I reached the top, and my courage, which had begun to fade, was rekindled, propelling me toward the glowing marble passageway, a brass chandelier illuminating it with the glow of daylight.

There was the door to the ballroom, intricately carved in whimsical relief, in a profuse indiscriminateness of tragic monsters and gods. I walked on. Doubt continued to assail me: how would I open the door? But once in front of it, I gave it just the slightest push and felt it give way, slide, and swing gently on its doorjamb, allowing me free passage into the ballroom, which glowed in stunning resplendency.

The columns were flaming cylinders, sparkling and emitting the fiery glow of burning logs; the moldings glowed; the floor, covered by a flame-colored carpet, seemed to curdle like burning lava, rising in waves of thick smoke that permeated the air with warm, stupefying fragrance.

Incense burners emitted blue spirals, and they were endless in number—tall, on strange tripods whose narrow legs rested on clawed feet.

A bronze pyre burned in the middle of the ballroom in cerulean flames, one minute as a single pyramidal flame and the next in fragmented, flickering tongues.

Suddenly, I shuddered. I was being followed and watched. I stopped, my heart struck with fear, feeling breathless and choking. I looked around and then recognized my own image in the silent follower—which was not one, as it first seemed, but many, reproduced in all the mirrors that faced each other, widening and deepening the size of the ballroom indefinitely, uniformly multiplying the golden columns, the tripods, the burning pyre, the furniture, and my image; every movement.

I ventured over to the hidden door tucked into a recessed arch. I pushed it, and it gave way without a sound, opening into a sort of fragrant-smelling, bluish crypt from whose vaulted ceiling hung a shell-shaped candelabra, radiating pale, flickering flames from its seven nozzles. My feet sank softly into the fluffy fur rug, and so thick was the air that moving through it required the effort of a swimmer breaking through the body of the waves.

But the glow of a fiery furnace lit the end of the passage. I steered myself hastily toward it, almost in a run, and came out in a circular enclosure like the inside of a dome, draped in mourning by a funereal purple light, filtered through porcelain vials.

Carved out like grottoes in the walls were strange niches lined with violet silk and embroidered with silver lilies, guarding sparkling-eyed idols.

An enormous golden chandelier hung from the center, suspended by a shimmering scaled serpent. Scattered all around were bronze bowls, crackling with aromatic resins, or large onyx and alabaster urns holding fading bouquets of flowers. On a low bed, at whose head a human-sized Buddha kept vigil, was a body covered by a delicate diaphanous veil.

I raised it ever so slightly, and by just lifting one end, it rippled and curled like mist in the wind.

I uncovered the entire body and, with a violent shudder, recoiled in horror, recognizing the corpse as Arhat.

The funereal light shone in full on his livid and hollowed face, baring his shriveled hands, his eyes sunken into their sockets, and exacerbating the point of his chin.

I was overcome by terror—my spirit was fading, and my body surrendered, collapsing beside the coffin.

I staggered, my knees buckling in a cowardly exhaustion. I clutched an urn.

Ominous noises rumbled, perhaps it was the wind moaning outside or . . . who knows? I picked myself up, and, unsteadily groping my way, unable to see in the sepulchral glow of that death chamber, I walked stiffly, colliding with the walls, and reaching the vaulted passage, I took off running in terror.

As I came out of the ballroom, I was blinded by the bright light. I reached the passageway and dashed down the stairs at breakneck speed before crossing the hall.

When I reached my chamber, I stretched out my arms, rushing to the door as if to break it down, and lunged into the void.

The door opened and, in the middle of the room, in full light, stood Arhat, staring and motionless, sinister.

The afternoon was fading when I stopped work and stretched out on the divan to rest. My interest in the manuscript, far from growing with the, admittedly curious, developments the "novel" was taking, dwindled into nothing more than literary curiosity. It was not a truthful account as I had assumed but instead a fantasy, a work of pure fiction, woven with a certain ingenuity into a dazzling fable.

The Englishman had enjoyed himself at my expense by offering me his literature enveloped in a mystery.

Ultimately, it was always meant to be a distraction in my spare time, and if it did not put me at the threshold of the arcane, it certainly showed me, in full light, the brilliant imagination of a romantic.

It was getting dark. The cicadas were singing in concert. Suddenly, I felt a jolt, as if the house had been suspended from its foundation, and then a loud boom, followed by a thunderous rattle, then another, and another . . .

The nearby quarry was the source of the tremendous mine explosion, dislodging blocks of stones, veritable boulders that rolled thunderously down the hillside, that often brought with them coconut palms, old trees, and layers of earth covered with undergrowth, crushing them against the edges of the monstrous jagged rock.

I got dressed, and the shadows had already begun to darken the corners when I lit the gas lamps and went downstairs for dinner.

The bright dining room, with its chairs around the flowered table set with china and sparkling crystal, was still deserted. The guests began to appear on the veranda, walking through the garden.

Brandt, always alone, absorbed in his dreams, listened closely to the ancient rhythms, the soft expression of dead melodies. He came and went slowly along the cool rows of trees, circling the flower beds, moist from watering, and brushed by the new roses that leaned languidly on their stems, already experiencing an outpouring of nocturnal voluptuousness.

At times he would stop, reach out to a branch, and take a leaf between his fingers, rolling it and crushing it, his eyes lost in the moment, absorbed as if following a dream that dissipates sweetly in the ether before vanishing and becoming one with the night like other dreams.

Basílio, hunched in a wicker chair, was squinting with his beady eyes at something to sharpen his sarcasm. Carlos and Eduardo were whispering together at the railing; Crispim was whistling softly as he leaned against a doorway.

The house had a melancholy air, a certain gloominess hovered over it, clouding its normal liveliness; its mood was different: upset, downcast, and weary.

The Commander and Pericles appeared. Basílio, noticing them, turned completely around in the chair.

"So? Will she, or won't she?"

"It looks bad," said the Commander.

"Oh, that disease . . . and the doctor?" The old man shrugged his shoulders. Curiosity gathered all the lodgers into a group, and the bookkeeper, looking at Pericles, asked:

"Have you gone to see her?"

"No," he said, flinching. "Penalva is there. He understands. Not me. What can I do?"

"A quick photograph, man. The stage is set."

"Nonsense . . . !" muttered Pericles, turning his back.

The dinner bell sounded, and we all went inside. Miss Barkley appeared unchanged, nodded her head, and took her place. The servant brought in the soup and, in silence, respectful of the rite, dinner began.

Penalva wore a more serious expression, the stern composure of a man full of responsibilities. Everyone knew the doctor had asked him for help, entrusting him with the patient, making him the caretaker of that life he felt was slipping away little by little, despite his efforts to sustain it in that weak and fragile body.

"Well, Doctor?" asked Basílio . . . "Miss Fanny?" The student pursed his lips. Brandt turned to look at him.

"Have you no hope?"

"Hope? She's lost," he concluded, stuffing a hunk of bread into his mouth. Miss Barkley took a deep breath and reached to arrange some roses in the vase.

"What struck me is the hallucination."

"Hallucination?" exclaimed the Commander.

"Yes, hallucination," Penalva insisted. Brandt's eyes widened and he asked:

"Hallucination?"

"Yes, it's true. Last night, no sooner had the doctor left when the hallucinatory state began to manifest itself. She was lying quietly in bed, seemingly asleep when suddenly, trembling, she sprang up with a start and sat up, her eyes wide open, staring at the back of the room. We tried to get her to lie back down, but she gently pushed us away, exhibiting the same agitated state, very pale, quite cold and trembling. She stayed like that for a moment until she covered her face with her hands and began sobbing, falling back onto the bed as if abandoned."

"It was Mr. James," said Miss Barkley. There was a commotion at the table, and several voices exclaimed in the same surprise, "Mr. James?!"

"Yes," said the Englishwoman calmly. Everyone then set down their cutlery, bending forward to listen as they lapped up her words, and in the anxious silence, she continued, pausing:

"Yes, Mr. James. That's what she told me. She saw him at the head of the bed, well, not the man himself, but a young woman who had his face, wearing a tunic like a statue."

The words of the Englishwoman sent a chill down my spine, my hair stood on end, and my skin itched with irritation.

"Poor thing!" concluded Miss Barkley. Glances were exchanged, and dinner continued on in silence. Basílio burst forth in a fit of scorn, however:

"So . . . wearing a tunic? Woman . . . ?" Miss Barkley nodded her head. "Because, look, that's nothing new. Although I never saw him in a tunic like a statue, I always thought of him as being of the other sex." Miss Barkley's spectacles flashed. "I'm sorry, Miss, but it's the truth." And excitedly pulling his napkin from his collar, he exclaimed, "Is that the face of a man?" He looked around at the group. "If police had been here, I guarantee we would have already gotten to the bottom of the case. Because after all, who knows? Russia is full of women anarchists, and they're worse than men. Anyway . . . I'd best shut up. Let them sneak up on us!" He seized upon his roast beef, furiously stabbing at the slice of meat that bloodied his lettuce-laden plate.

Brandt looked at him with contempt and said not a word until the end of dinner, pecking slowly and distractedly at his food with his fork. Now and again the corners of his mouth creased in a fleeting hint of a smile.

Basílio raged indignantly against the beauty of James, with the outraged revulsion of a puritan in the face of obscene depravity.

When we got up from the table, Brandt, grabbing my arm, asked in a hushed voice:

"Do you have anything to do?"

"No."

"Come with me. That man irritates me, he tortures my nerves!" And he glanced at the bookkeeper, who was getting his fill of spreading hatred on the veranda.

We left. The musician was silent until we reached his cottage, absentmindedly stroking his thin moustache.

The sitting room was dark and stuffy. Brandt opened wide the windows, and the curtains fluttered in the breeze.

In the glow of the gas, the whole artistic ensemble of the interior emerged from the shadows: lacquers and laminates sparkled; flowers bloomed anew in the light; paintings in wide frames of gold and lacquer or waxed wood depicted landscapes of faraway countrysides, hardy wheat, inlets, woods, and cattle; and the sad storks on the partition screen seemed to ruffle their feathers, such was the luminosity of their gold and silk threads. Brandt leaned against the piano, and holding a cigarette between his fingers, swinging his leg, he became pensive. I sank into an armchair, smoking. Gusts of damp wind shook the branches of the flowerless jasmine tree.

The sad night was gloomy and warm, a cavernous darkness weighing heavy.

"My dear fellow," said the musician, "extraordinary things are happening in this house. Things that are truly astonishing."

"Why?"

"Did you hear what Miss Barkley said about Miss Fanny's vision?"

"Yes, James . . ."

"Well, my friend, I'm not sick, nor could one say that I've been affected by this or that, because only this morning did I learn about the teacher's illness. Last night, however—it was around one perhaps—finishing my work, I leaned out the window, just looking around, and saw a figure appear on the veranda, pause for a second, and then slowly go down the steps, crossing a row of acacia trees to the jasmine arch, where it stopped. The figure was wearing a diaphanous white tunic, whose surface glimmered with cerulean light. At first, I thought it was the teacher, even though she seemed attired rather lavishly to my eyes, and to convince myself, I went out into the garden. The figure remained in position. I rushed forward, and about ten steps away, I felt frozen, as if covered in snow. I stopped, stared, and in the specter recognized . . ."

"James."

Brandt nodded his head and confirmed:

"James."

"And then?"

"The jasmine tree took on a whiteness, like a mysterious moonlight that shone on it alone, but the paleness sort of rippled, rising in a light breeze, and then faintly faded away. It hovered a moment over the arch, shrinking back and then swelling before it rose softly, then swiftly, as if carried away by a strong wind, and disappeared . . . I saw it!"

He lit a cigarette before sitting down on the piano bench, his gaze unfocused and lost.

"Well, my dear Frederico, the same thing happened to me. I wouldn't have said anything if you hadn't told me about your vision. The same thing happened to me, at nearly the same time." And I described the apparition that had emerged in the darkness of the hall.

"What do you think?"

"Me? I don't know. You don't believe in collective hallucinations, do you?"

"I neither believe nor doubt: life is a mystery, and I am alive. That Englishwoman, who I've always liked, since I felt she was unhappy, is one of those loving spirits who only lives to love. Withdrawn in virtue, she expands in kindness. She is a virgin tree covered with flowers, sterilizing herself in their fragrance. Fruit is of the earth, and fragrance is of space. Apparently, it is an inert force but . . . The rose is a delicacy, a cluster of oysters whose pearl is the scent . . . And the rose poisons and kills just as love does. Miss Fanny crawls, enslaved to James, and he, who knows? That apparition coinciding with the Englishwoman's illness . . ."

"And could it be him?"

"Who else could it be?"

"But in that case, he died . . ."

"Why?"

"Because only the dead appear."

"But the spirit is immortal, my friend. Just as thought is one's true north, one's will is one's energy. He who is able to focus so much that he becomes absorbed into himself immortalizes matter by impregnating it with eternity. The acts that we call unconscious are products of creative minds, an energy that does not rest like intelligence, subordinated to matter, but surrounds it, circling it like the sun.

"The brain represents a lamp, and intelligence represents the wick—the spark that ignites it is inspiration, the *mens*[24] I alluded to, which is the very essence of life, and that essence, all too often repudiated when it manifests itself inappropriately, is what we call—idea. If our eyes were not prepared exclusively to view matter, we would see the environment and understand the truth, and all the false notions that confuse us—starting with that vacuum we call time—would disappear like specters scattered by the sun.

---

24. The Latin word *mens*, which translates as "mind," is the origin of English words like *mental* and *dementia*.

"The dead do not manifest themselves. What we call dead is the corpse, the remains. A tunic cannot be worn correctly unless it is fitted to the body. If matter is contained in sleep, the spirit can leave without life ceasing to sustain it with its dynamics.

"Steer a skiff to port, a boatman rigs the sail, secures the oars, removes the rudder, ties it up, and jumps ashore. The boat continues to be lashed by the crashing waves. If the cable that holds it happens to break, the boat pulls away, drifts, or capsizes, but if the mooring holds, the boat awaits the return of its owner, who reinstalls his gear and guides the boat out toward the open sea."

"Life is the sea, the boat is the body, and the boatman is the soul.

"Do you remember Genesis? It's right there in the second verse: 'And the Spirit of God moved upon the face of the waters.' It was the absolute soul, the eternal fecundity, hovering, procreative, over the still motionless sea of universal life. Jesus lived among fishermen—souls. Is the storm on Lake Tiberias[25] not the representation of life's turmoil? And didn't Christ, spurning the boat, walk on the water in front of his disciples? Why? What for? To show that the Spirit of God does not need a body."

---

25. A freshwater lake in Israel also called the Sea of Galilee, Kinneret, or Kinnereth.

For a long time, we were quiet with our thoughts. Then Brandt stood up in front of me and, with eyes blazing, whispered, as if he was afraid of being overheard, "My dear man, science is a spiral column, always spinning. It seems to us as if the spirals are moving upward, increasing in height . . . but unfortunately, this is nothing but an illusion, pure illusion, isn't it true? We get as far as the cornice of the temple, from there up is the great void, and the spirals spin and spin . . .

"We talk about progress and fall into death. Nothing is known. I consider music to be the most spiritual of the arts, because music is pure essence. Rhythm is its law, sound is its manifestation of the nature of light and the heavens; simple vibration, ethereal wave, nothing more. Somehow, music explains the invisible to me, and I understand the soul when I perform. I feel God when I compose."

"You?"

"Yes, me. All artists descend from the ideal to the real. The musician ascends; he leaves the realm of the real for the ideal. Poetry compresses thought into words, sculpture is stone or metal, architecture is plaster, painting is paint—music is rhythm and sound: the indefinite.

"Sound is like the smoke from incense burners—a winged prayer.

"In ancient temples, alongside the incense burners echoed the lyres and the waves, as twins they rose together in flight—those of fragrance rose into clouds; those of sound rose into melodies. A poem is what it is—ideas arranged in layers; a statue is a copy of still life; a building is a set of inflexible lines; a painting is a vision of one point in space in the light of a sunbeam. A song is breath and soul, and as a soul it is essence.

"Life is a rhythm that unfolds in recurrent patterns just as the wave multiplies in undulations."

Throwing his hand up at random, he hit a note on the piano—the sound vibrated, echoed, faded out, and died.

He raised his arm and, with a straight finger, made a piercing motion, murmuring, "The spiral . . . the spiral . . ."

He went over to the window and was quiet for a moment, immersing his eyes in the darkness outside. But then, he turned around and continued. "The apparition didn't frighten me, it excited me like a proclamation of truth. It was a flash of lightning that gave me a glimpse of the beyond. But let's focus on the music. The other day you said when talking about Beethoven that you admired him but did not understand him."

"Yes. Much of what is heralded as the beauty of symphonies goes unnoticed by me."

"It's only natural. Imagine if you arrived in a theocratic country and were soon taken to a temple where the most solemn religious ceremony was being celebrated in all its grandeur. You would see the inside of that majestic building, the splendor of its marble, gold, and stone; you would see colossal idols on sumptuous altars; you would see the resplendent priests performing mysterious movements in hushed tones; you would see the virgin priestesses dancing to the sound of the bronze sistrums; you would hear the prayers of the multitude and be simply dazzled, but you would not feel mystical emotion because you did not understand the words of the prayers, what the dances represented, the value of the rituals—in short, the rite itself. In contrast, if you had been initiated into the esoteric symbols—that is, the 'intrinsic reasons' behind the rites—your enlightened spirit would understand the beauty and significance of the most subtle acts, and you would attain the ideal truth. Music is like that.

"It is not enough to just hear it; it has to be understood, felt, interpreted. One has to have both the emotion and the knowledge. Beethoven's symphonies have not a single excess note, just like a leafy tree has not a single useless leaf.

"Music is a seemingly easy language, yet it is the most difficult of all. There are seven notes, some on lines as if touching the ground, and others in space, hovering: reptiles and birds, grass and clouds, flowers and stars. Seven are the values, seven the rests, seven the accidentals, seven the keys, and three, the types of beat. It's not much, and yet it's everything. All the voices and sounds fit on the staff. There are five chords, and they are enough: in them whispers the subtle breeze and thunders the storm's fury.

"All of nature's harmonies are contained within the confines of the pentagram."

He went over to the window, staring out, absorbed in silence.

The branch of the jasmine tree swayed gently as if beckoning, stretching to reach him.

A moth flitted around the gas nozzle. Brandt made not the slightest gesture, absorbed as he was, dreaming, immobilized in thought as if on the edge of an abyss.

"What's the matter, Frederico?" I asked in concern, and he, as if surprised, turned around, his eyes misty and pale, and, lifting his hand to his brow to push aside his hair, murmured faintly:

"I don't know . . . I don't know . . ." He opened the piano and sat down, with his hands flat on the keys, where he paused, entranced. Suddenly, he stood up and began walking around the room with his head down, repeating in a muffled voice, "I don't know."

He stopped in front of me, staring, distracted:

"I look crazy, don't I? If you could only imagine what I feel . . . Music makes me crazy. Wagner was right—'it is literally the revelation of another world.' And I feel so much, so intensely! . . . Inspiration flows to me in torrents, but because I have so many ideas, they get trampled trying to get into my head, like an agitated swarm of bees, jumbled up in a ball at the narrow opening of the beehive. You can't imagine how horrible it is! Fecundity in excess is like a flood in the river, it is like a plethora in the veins—it overwhelms and suffocates."

At that moment, a figure appeared at the window, pushing aside the jasmine branch, and both Brandt and I reacted with the same surprise. It was Penalva. The fifth-year student, noticing our jitters, looked at us confused:

"Am I interrupting something?"

"No. Come in. Let's talk." He begged off: "I've been at the bedside of Miss Fanny. I came only to pass on a request from the patient."

"A request? And how is she?"

"Bad. Another hemoptysis."[26]

Brandt insisted. "Come in." It was drizzling.

He went to open the door for him. The student came in but did not accept the seat offered by the musician. No, he couldn't stay long. And with a feeble smile:

26. Coughing up of blood.

"She asked if you could play a little organ music." Brandt's eyes sparkled and a pasty pallor covered his face:

"Poor thing!" he lamented, shaken. He opened the lid of the organ and wiped the keyboard with his handkerchief.

He eagerly opened the windows and doors so that the sound could pass in unfettered waves. Penalva headed out the door, saying his goodbyes from the threshold:

"Good night!"

"Why in such a hurry, man!"

"She's bad off and may not make it to the morning. Miss Barkley is there but . . . See you tomorrow." And he went running into the trees. The organ throbbed at the pressure of the pedals operated by Brandt.

"So?" exclaimed the musician, with a questioning nod of his head.

"What?"

"This request. What do you think?"

"Romanticism." He smiled, bending over the instrument, and soon a very soft sound developed into a suggestive melody, and, with his head held high, he said:

"Music, my friend, is a religion for those who feel it."

"What is this?" I asked, delighted.

"The theme song of the fatal passion of *Tristan and Isolde*."[27] He stopped, grabbing an album of music and leafing through it, and opening it on the stand, he announced, "Bach's *Prelude in E-Flat Minor*. It's as good as Genesis, my friend. Listen. It's quite a piece."

He sat back down, pausing for a moment before throwing back his head and staring up. Then, leaning over the keyboard, he hit the first chord.

Outside there was a thunderous beating in the foliage, a flurry of rustling branches. Windows rattled in a mighty gust. Lightning flashed eerily.

But the somber sounds rose like a prayer into the night. From a distance came sullen rumbles of thunder, and the sweeping phrases, original as untouched nature, unfolded and grew wide, and the impression they made on my soul was of a chorus of sorrowful voices mysteriously chanting in the sinister space.

Howling winds lingered through the night, from moment to moment interspersed by flashes of light. Suddenly the musician froze, then stood up nervously and glanced around.

---

27. Gottfried von Strassburg's thirteenth-century version of the medieval romance of Tristan and Isolde, based on Celtic legend, is considered the masterpiece of medieval German poetry and was the basis for Richard Wagner's opera *Tristan und Isolde* (*Tristan and Isolde*), first performed in 1865.

"What is it?" The rain intensified, brutalizing the leaves in downpours. Brandt went to the window, pushing aside the branch of the jasmine tree as he closed the shutter, but paused, hesitantly. Again, the loose branch poked itself into the room, swaying as the musician stepped back to the organ.

"Why don't you close the window?"

He shook his head no and, through the divine music, spoke as if in a dream:

"What does it matter! Perhaps she asked me to play to put her to sleep."

And, over the roar of the torrential rain, the sounds of the organ, at times sorrowful, filled the night with human anguish.

V

Despite Brandt's insistence that I stay, I decided to brave the stormy weather, returning to the shelter of my room, drenched from head to toe, and, until late into the night, claps of thunder seemed to explode on the roof while rain poured down incessantly.

In the darkness of my room, where lightning insinuated itself through the crevices and ignited vivid outbursts, the sound of the constant swoosh of overflowing water and the stiff gusts of wind added to the violence and noise.

I dozed off, enjoying the soft comfort of my bed, under the safety of my rooftop.

In the morning, while on my way downstairs to bathe, I heard the news that Miss Fanny had died. Pericles, who was on his way up, wearing his jupon and carrying his soap holder and sponge, his hair tangled, had asked sadly:

"Have you heard?" And, in the face of my speechless surprise, he announced, "The Englishwoman . . . she passed! At five this morning."

A bitter taste of distress bubbled in my throat, and I uttered not a word. We stared at each other, and a distraught Pericles, frowning and shaking his head, snatched up his jupon, exposing his thin, hairy legs, and slowly continued up the stairs, murmuring mournfully.

In the dining room, Basílio, already dressed in a raincoat down to his ankles, was breakfasting at the table. Catching sight of me, he opened wide his puffy eyes and, throwing back his last sip, stood up, stepping over gingerly in his galoshes to secretly whisper:

"So, eh? What did I tell you?" But his big, wrinkled face was sullen as he said with concern, "Now all we can do is wait for the consequences. We'll have the health department here. It won't be long before they'll come with their acids and their infernal burners. It will be a disaster! During the time of the bubonic, that bubonic plague caused by the rats,"[28] he gestured with his hand to denote stealing, "I lived on Rua de São José. A fellow there died, and they declared the place infested . . . Well, my friend, the folks from the department ransacked the house, and let me tell you! I ended up with not a single pair of briefs to change into. Now, just imagine . . . ! I have a new frock coat I haven't even worn. You then . . . It's not for a lack of

28. Brazil's first reported outbreak of plague occurred 18 October 1899. The bacteria was identified in samples taken from sick patients in the São Paulo port city of Santos (Read).

charity, but these things, in a house full of people like this . . . Hospitals were not meant for dogs. Let me tell you: if I get sick, send me to my fraternal order. There, I have everything whenever I want it. I'm comfortable and I don't owe anyone any favors. And then what . . . consumption! Wherever it goes, it stays, it's like bedbugs. If I had the time, I'd move. Are you going to the funeral?"

"I don't know."

Basílio clucked his tongue: "Don't go, man. It's a different religion. I'm not going. I don't go into cemeteries, too many foreigners. No reason, it's a question of principle. That's not for the living. I'll have to go when they carry me off, but by my own two feet, never. Not to cemeteries nor to masses."

As he spoke, steadying his foot on the edge of a chair, he folded the hem of his trousers. Then he picked up his umbrella, shook it with disgust, and exclaimed, "Beastly weather!" He lit a cigarette and, lifting the collar of his raincoat, tiptoed away, cautiously, stealthily, afraid of someone calling him back for something.

Crossing the corridor on my way back from the bath, I saw Brandt standing at the door of the cottage, still dressed in his pajamas, gazing thoughtfully at the trees, covered in rain, dripping sadly like humble weeping.

As he saw me, he extended his arms, raising them in a gesture of consternation. Then he stepped through the doorway, wrinkling his brow as the rain sprayed his face, asking:

"Are you going to the funeral?"

"I don't know. Are you?"

He stepped back as the wind drove the drizzle toward the door and, from the middle of the room, said more loudly, "It'll be tough. I have a lesson in Niteroi today. Well . . . maybe. What time?"

"Four o'clock, naturally."

He paused for a second, thinking as he twisted a strand of hair curled over his forehead. Finally he decided:

"I'll go. We should go. Take a coach. Let's go together." And he said goodbye: "I'll see you later."

At lunch, Miss Barkley wrote the obituary for the deceased woman, describing her virtuous life from the day Miss Barkley had fetched her from aboard the *Danube* to that sad morning.

> She came from a Puritan family from Scotland. Her father was a professor at Oxford, and she, the youngest of eight children who had all scattered, grew up, always frail and restrained, among taciturn scholars and rigidly austere Quakers, moving from scientific controversies to detailed commentary on the Bible, from Luther's hymns to the sweet songs of the highlanders, who at night, in the dining hall,

would reminisce about their homeland, old folks and family friends sitting around the table or fire, chanting in mystical tones as if invoking the deities of the hills, offering up, in nostalgic song, the sacrifice of another day spent in the land of exile.

She had acquired a solid education and, at the age of eighteen, left her father's home for Australia as a governess. There she lived for three years and then, in need of sunshine, came to Brazil, where, after five years of constant work, she succeeded in making an honest name for herself, always surrounded by children who numbed the wistfulness in her heart and the thoughts of her soul with the joyful sounds of their merrymaking and the pure delight of their smiles. She was a young woman of virtue! Of such virtue!

Penalva, who had strayed not a minute from the bedside of Miss Fanny, spoke of her gentle death: "She clasped her hands together and closed her eyes as if to sleep. There was not a single tremble or breath. She was dead."

The Commander drew in a breath and uttered with feeling, "Poor girl!" The servant dished up the beef in silence. The velvety sound of a bell toll echoed somberly in the misty air, while the clock jangled, announcing the time in joyful timbre.

A scuffling of feet could be heard out on the veranda, accompanied by the snapping of closing umbrellas and the whispered murmur of voices, and at the door to the room, as if on a school holiday, a group of blond children dressed in white appeared, wide-eyed and inquisitive, each carrying bouquets of flowers.

Miss Barkley stood up to welcome them. The children were followed by the severe visages of heartsick servants dressed in aprons and bonnets.

They filed in slowly, guiding the bewildered children.

The scent of flowers floated sweetly in the air as if emanating from a garden, and the group slipped into a line, disappearing into the tiny mortuary room.

The Commander confessed that he was truly sorry for that "catastrophe": "So young, poor thing . . ."

Penalva asked if he had gone to see her. The old man slapped his hand over his eyes as if repulsed by a horrifying vision, his face bathed in a grimace of disgust:

"No. I don't like to see dead people, it's too shocking, and when one reaches a certain age, one should avoid such displays. If a rainy day like this one makes me nervous, imagine a dead young woman. No! I prefer the sun, the hustle and bustle, life," and he leaned over his cup of coffee, slurping it down.

Penalva made mention of the beauty of the deceased: "She looks like marble, Commander, even her freckles have faded. She's beautiful!" The old man looked at him with wild eyes, and the student went on: "Yes sir, beautiful! There are women like that, it's as if they were made for the tomb: ugly in life, they become beautiful in death. There was a case like that at school." And he went on to describe it: "One young girl while sick in the hospital was hideous. Hours after she died, though, it was as if a scaly mask had been peeled off to reveal the smooth delicate skin of a fifteen-year-old, surprising everyone with her beauty. People crowded into the amphitheater to see her. Décio wrote her a sonnet; a wonderful sonnet!"

"Come now!" cried the Commander, incredulous.

"I assure you it was so!" confirmed Penalva, seriously.

"Well, my friend, in any case, I prefer life." We all got up, and each retreating to his own room, the house fell silent in the veiled light of the gloomy day, beneath the drizzle that spread a flitting trickle into the air like a cloud of mosquitoes over a vast mudhole.

The day faded and became oppressive. The feeble light of dull sunshine passed through a few openings in the clouds. Faint thunder rolled lazily from a distance, and flies, invading the stuffy interior, flitted impertinently, pursuing each other in lazy fury as they buzzed monotonously, making the warm, muffled silence even more noticeable.

I tried to work but was distracted by thoughts of the dead woman's chamber.

A whiff of fragrance invaded my room as if it had come from that funereal room, and then, against a blurred, dreamlike background, it appeared to take the shape of the corpse of the Englishwoman as Penalva had described her, framed in roses and white lilies, her hands folded and clasped tightly together in prayerful devotion, a beatific smile stamped on her face.

I randomly opened the mysterious thick volume James had loaned me and began looking at the cryptographic scrawl that filled it: swirled lines, discs, spirals, urn shapes, crescents set between cross-shaped quotation marks, magical symbols, animal silhouettes like in Egyptian hieroglyphs. And as I idly flipped through it, distractedly, I reached the last page that had a drawing of a flower—a green stem held one lily upright, and the other was withered and limp, just like in the frontispiece.

There was no longer any doubt—it was a symbol that encapsulated the entire mystery of that obscure composition.

I focused my eyes on the bizarre figures, and whether it was an illusion due to fatigue or fantastic truth, all the characters slowly began to move—the spirals uncoiled, lengthening like torpid snakes reanimated through gentle warmth; the discs bulged, growing into orbs and rising on the page like iridescent soap bubbles; the urns stood upright; the crescents were illuminated with a glimmer of moonlight on the black crosses that expanded by extending both sides of their unbending arms; the various symbols twirled in a dizzying spin; and the multiplying animals, growing larger, arched their backs, spread their bristly or scruffy-feathered wings, their gleaming eyes blazing in combat, and fled, prancing or escaping in terrified flight, dissolving like rings of smoke fading into the air. I rubbed my bewildered eyes for a long time. Then, turning the page, I saw everything in its original and normal state. It was just an illusion!

I got up to walk around the room in an attempt to repel the dark thoughts that washed over me.

Why was my spirit bothered by that persistent thought of death? The corpse that I felt suspended above me, floating, stiff and cold, white, among the flowers, why must it follow me?

I could see things clearly around me yet perceived nothing, nothing! But the dead woman was with me, enveloping me, harassing me.

In the sharp brightness of the mirrors, there was at times a darkening, a cloud that would briefly obscure the dazzling clarity. It was nothing more than a reflection of the sky, gloomy then suddenly clear as the sun wavered.

I threw myself onto the bed, spent, unable to rid myself of the thoughts of that morning's demise, that soul that left the land of the suffering to enter the bosom of mystery. I wanted to follow it, see it change into the light, become part of the infinite brightness, and I just stared. Feeling sleepy, however, I tried to rouse myself to call Alfredo and ask him to order the carriage, but such was my fatigue that I could not even sit up, and soon I fell back onto the pillows, falling asleep immediately.

An icy hand lightly touched my forehead and squeezed my hand, which hung over the side of the bed, and as I opened my eyes in fright, I saw a misty shape, a delicate, diaphanous body, undulating like the reflection of fog in rippling waters, flowing away in silent movement.

I sat up suddenly, rattled and haunted. I walked fearfully through the room, looking around—it was deserted. My brass clock on the desk indicated precisely three o'clock.

Had it been a warning? Her? Asking for my company so she would not have to travel alone through those streets under the inclement sadness of a winter sky, she who had come for the sunshine, seeking out the vital and beautiful light of our days?

Could it be? I called Alfredo and, on edge, heard no more than the sound of footsteps in the corridor when I ran to the door to give him the message:

"Please call for a carriage. Hurry! Is it always at four o'clock?"

"Yes, sir."

"Has Brandt already arrived?"

"I think so because the cottage is open."

"Then go. Get a coupé." I splashed water on my face and began to dress, troubled by the sensation that had awakened me.

Standing in front of the mirror without seeing myself, I thought, Oh, my nerves! My poor excited nerves were beginning to loosen in cowardly indifference. Undoubtedly, I needed to react. My soul, seized by the terror, weakened benignly at the simplest of events: the flight of an insect that landed on the windowpane caused me to shudder; the cracking of furniture made my blood run cold. I gave a sharp tug to the lapel of my frock coat and walked to the window.

The sun was breaking through the thinning clouds, and the air was fresh and mild. Large swathes of blue appeared, and the lustrous foliage shone tenderly like yesterday's shoots. A few errant raindrops fell sporadically.

I went downstairs. In the parlor, two Englishmen were smoking idly, and a boy, dressed in a sailor suit, leaned against the table, leafing through a copy of *Graphic*.[29]

I walked to the veranda, intending to go to the cottage, when Brandt entered the parlor, still smoothing down the wrinkled sleeves of his frock coat.

---

29. This is likely a reference to *National Geographic*, the first issue of which was published in 1888.

"Is it time?"

"Yes."

Miss Barkley appeared; spoke to the Englishmen, who then got up; and advised us as well: "Everything was ready. They went to close the coffin. If you wish . . ." We accompanied her.

Atop a narrow table in the middle of the room lay the black coffin, covered with a veneer of silver branches. Several women bustled around it, arranging the flowers, stuffing them into openings, and the dead woman, very white, looked like wax. Her cheeks were hollowed as the bones protruded; her eyes were sunken, half-open as if unbuttoned in the purpleness of their sockets; her nose was very tapered; and her thin, colorless lips were cracked and dry. A few strands of blond hair brightened her smooth forehead. Clutched in her ivory hands were dying flowers, and a tiny gold cross rested on her flat bosom.

They closed the coffin without tears. The Englishmen grabbed and lifted it like a simple bundle; Brandt and I helped them. Then we left.

The women came out onto the veranda. We passed through the lush rose bushes whose dangling branches dripped onto the coffin. One of the flowers was shedding its petals, and as the gardener slowly opened wide the gate, a fair cicada on the arbor let loose a gay, summery song, happy with the sun coming out into the blue sky, free as a flagged vessel opening wide its sails to the wind, as it gracefully navigated the calm seas, far from the mist, far from the chilly reefs, far from the snow-white rocks, through the peaceful serenity of smooth waters.

The people of the neighborhood stood by their windows, and the sidewalks were full of the curious. Miss Barkley waited while the last straps were secured, and when the horse-drawn wagon carrying the coffin moved away, she waved her hand as simply as one saying goodbye to someone heading out for a night of enjoyment or a radiant morning of a never-ending day.

As we approached Rua Marquez de Abrantes, we crossed paths with the health department cart and a wagon carrying the disinfectants. I smiled, remembering the angry words of Basílio. Brandt murmured:

"The exorcism." And, after a pause, he added mysteriously, "If men could do the same to the heart, by ridding it of longing, the soul would suffer less in its brief journey on Earth.

"Death is the flower of the Tree of Life: wilted on the vine, it sheds its leaves, but is reborn through its pollen. The man who tills is not content to pull out little plants as he ploughs and weeds the field: he digs, uprooting the vines and the slightest trace of roots, and even sets fire to the stubble so that no nefarious seed is left. Here goes the flower. Poor flower! And there go the destroyers of the lethal germs she left scattered in her tiny room."

"Do you believe, Brandt?"

"I believe, yes. I do, even though I think death is nothing more than an ascension—what we call life is the purification of the self. Nature, that's all. The soul comes into existence as if on a scale of perfection, passing from the least to the greatest, oscillating between good and evil. The vague memory of a previous life exists in all men, and there is a propensity toward the beyond: the earth holds us back, heaven attracts us. Death is the victory of the absolute.

"We were once trees, a spurt made us birds, and instead of captivating roots, we acquired loose, space-conquering wings. Today men, tomorrow . . ."

"Poetry . . ."

"Poetry is the flower of truth, my friend, although all the ideas that stand out from the ordinary, the superior and the imbecilic, are, due to misunderstanding or contempt, despicably bestowed.

"Poets are clairvoyant: they use symbols to announce what will happen in the days to come. A flower has no taste but, rather, only a scent: a line of poetry is pure abstraction—soul. Fruit, with its tasty flesh, comes later to the tree.

"Examine any scientific law and you will find in it the essence of poetry. The first sages were contemplatives: the word of Wisdom was born to the sound of lyres. Apollo guided Minerva's baby steps.[30] Everything is poetry."

The coupé slowed its pace in a jam of carriages, blocked by a wagon piled high with granite slabs, whose tall wheels had gotten stuck in the mud in front of the tangled scaffolding of a building under construction.

Whip cracks could be heard above the clamor of angry shouting. Finally, there was an excited cry, a yell of encouragement, and then the thundering sound of several vehicles starting off in different directions. And the onlookers flowed back, arguing. We continued on.

In front of the health department, Brandt observed:

"It is as if we've gone beyond the city gates. Notice how different everything is here: it has a different look and feel. Even the mud is black as if made of coal dust."

The street, cratered and curved, glimmered in a murky haze. We moved slowly along the great wharf, among trucks that bounced and jerked along, with a rattle of iron.

---

30. Minerva (the Roman counterpart of the Greek goddess Athena) is the daughter of Jupiter (the Roman counterpart of the Greek god Zeus) and sister of Apollo.

Grease-smeared coopers wearing leather aprons hammered staves and shaved fifths, and an acidic, vinegary odor emanated from a moldy vat.

Tanned and wrinkly skinned seafarers clad in smocks or shirtsleeves, their sturdy arms welted with turgid veins, congregated in groups at the doors of commercial establishments, smoking pipes or laughing loudly. In vast shadowy storehouses, piles of sacks wedged into narrow rows were stacked nearly to the ceilings.

In the sooty depths of the foundries there was a blazing of pyres, and the clang of iron could be heard over the rumble of machines.

Loaders loped along, bent over by the weight of their sacks, and, splashing in the mud, disappeared into decrepit row houses, and throngs of people, in a hurried back-and-forth, collided as they toiled or in their idleness: tattered women and ragged children sniffing around doors, enormous, bare-chested men, glistening with sweat, bursting in laughter, with their biceps bulging like huge vials of strength.

Alleys slanted upward, twisting at odd angles as we proceeded uphill through the flat houses with their crumbling tops, the edges of roofs covered in overgrowth, and, high above, on the rugged hillside, wretched hovels were erected in dovecotes—dumps, run-down shacks, and overcrowded huts, the remains of ruins from a dismantled shamble of a building collapse.

Tall obelisk chimneys snorted thick coils of dark smoke, and breaking through the din, from one moment to the next, was the howl of a hysterical yell or the echo of a foghorn.

When we reached the cemetery, we silently helped the two Englishmen remove the mud-spattered coffin from the carriage and, seizing the handles, slowly climbed the harsh rocky hillside between the thick, moisture-mucked wall and a winding row of bamboo.

The sun was shining brightly, free of the clouds that had fled in defeat. A soft breeze blew gently.

What a sad, lonely cemetery!

Haphazardly tucked against the hillside, here humped into ridges, there staggered onto steep slopes, blackened gravestones lay abandoned among a tangle of wild grass. The iron crosses were eroded by rust, the marble ones veined with black, desolate as death itself in that gloomy corner among shriveled and twisted trees, whose roots appeared exposed, orphans of the earth, carried away by the rain showers.

The summit, with a slender steeple poking out of the top, spilled its barren side into the cemetery. Straight ahead, the calm sea, accessed by a long bridge lined with wagons, sparkled with boats; and in the distance, encircling the smooth waters that were bluer than the sky itself, stood the lush mountains.

We reached the chapel—it was bare, with not a single symbol aside from the sad iron cross at the top of the pediment, among the swallows that fluttered by.

Inside, clerestory windows were set high up the white walls, and in the middle stood only the bier on which we rested the coffin.

The pastor, a pale man with a black beard and eyeglasses, awaited us, clad in a long-sleeved white robe, a black stole on his arm and a book between his hands.

He approached the coffin and began to read mechanically, in a voice that nearly faded out before rising suddenly in a harsh tone, as if summoning the divinity to receive the soul he offered.

It wasn't really a prayer, but rather a sort of transaction with the beyond, in which we could sense the merchant showing off the goods, praising them, and finally surrendering them with the annoyed frown of one who sells for less than he wanted. He closed his book and set off walking.

We followed him, carrying the light coffin up the hill to the ravine next to the wall, where the open grave of soft, pasty soil muddied to its bottom was waiting, guarded by gravediggers.

Again the pastor opened his book, murmured the prayer for the dead, and slowly, in a silence in which we could hear the languid rustle of branches, we lowered the coffin, which splashed in the emptiness of the soaked grave.

The shovel, passed from hand to hand, sounded five times as it dropped the earth on the coffin lid. We stepped away. Then, in their hurry to finish, the gravediggers took up their shovels in a deafening clatter.

The two Englishmen climbed to the top of the hill, and indifferent to the racket below, one extended his arm as he showed off the view, explaining it to his companion as he followed with his finger the twists and turns of the land, the coils of smoke from chimneys, the black roofs, the boats that glided away, the distant mountains, and even the clouds themselves. The other just stared.

In the sun-drenched branches, the cicadas sang cheerfully.

Brandt, in front of the chapel, as bare and desolate as if it had experienced the devastation of a slaughter, shook his head:

"No! I don't understand religion without ritual, nor ritual without pomp. Man needs to *see* in order to understand and love. It's not enough to just think about God, one needs to feel Him, see a tangible expression of Him before our eyes, as a target to which to pray, to which one can raise one's supplicating hands and let unleashed tears run in torrents."

"And nature? All of this? The earth and sky?"

"All this is creation, not God. And this chapel is a deserted house, a dead body that lacks . . ."

"An idol . . ."

"The soul, my friend, the soul of the religions, which is precisely poetry: an expression of kindness, love, hope, and faith . . . the symbol, the symbol, the eternal and necessary symbol.

"All this is distressingly sad, you must agree. Let's go!"

And we walked disconsolately down the steep hillside, heaped with stones.

Brandt hesitated a moment in front of the coupé. Finally, he said to the coachman, "To the club!"

And slumping down in his seat, exhausted, unburdening himself, he said, "I'm hungry! I've had quite a day. Fortunately, the sun is out. You can't imagine how bad I feel on these dark days." And, leaning over to look at the sky, he exclaimed in delight, "What a splendid afternoon!"

Scents and sounds living in the air insinuate themselves more than light does: the branch of a tree is an impediment to the sun—scents and sounds pass right through the thick walls of prisons.

They constantly assault our minds, visiting every twist and turn, they suggest ideas, awaken memories, generate ecstasies and terrors, arouse pleasure or provoke tears.

There are some melodies and scents that rekindle longing, while others allow our imaginations to completely take wing.

A garden in bloom inspires us as much as an orchestra does. And sounds can be harsh, just as smells can be bitter. The scent of violets is but a mumble, the flowering jasmine, a bacchanalian choir.

The sandalwood staff carried by the wine god Dionysus and his devotees should be adorned with gardenias and carnations.

When I came from the fresh night into the tepid confines of the house, I felt enveloped in the acrid smell of fumigation and acid. Stunned and confused, I strode through the silent gloom of the parlor, the low light of the vigil flame, crossed the corridor, and climbed the stairs to my quarters with the impression of having walked along the funerary passage of a burial chamber.

The telltale smell of death impregnated the entire house.

My small room reeked of it despite the open window. It was the mysterious "odor," fighting the remnants of death. Formidable fight between the poisons and the infinitesimals. Each atom was a battlefield.

And everywhere the battle waged.

As I undressed with the gas fully lit, I felt the fierce battle all around me. I imagined the exhalation of that corpse expanding, overtaking the house, invading every nook and cranny, poisoning the air, the water, the light, all of life's essences. But at the same time, the pungent odor that seemed to pique my sense of smell soothed me with the outlandish notion that, if the lethal principles permeating my own breath were bringing ruin to my innermost being, the armed adversaries were coming after them, and in the irritating smell that stung my membranes, I could feel their invisible spears, their swords with lunging stabs and blows, piercing with blade and tip, leaving not a single one alive—not even one—that would be enough to ravage my fragile body.

I lay down. In the darkness, however, the fight became more intense, and in the hallucinatory state in which I found myself, the sinister fantasy of my fearful delirium grew worse.

Before my eyes, in confusion blacker than darkness itself, throngs of troops passed by, and a noise, like anxious breathing, was the thunder of the clash that resumed.

My body teemed with itches—it was them, the enemies. At times, I felt suffocated, as if an iron lid were pressing down on my chest—it was the advance of the fierce hordes.

My eyes burned; my ears roared.

What a horrendous, formidable battle! And so must it have been throughout the house, in the open air and in the deepest cracks; at every point the invisibles treacherously lurked, waiting for the perfect moment for the assault. There went the fetid odor, with the deep breath of life, flushing out and devasting death.

I fell into a deep sleep, attempting to free myself from the horror of a harrowing nightmare. The dead woman appeared before me, immense and pale, as if illuminated by a halo of fleeting fires, naked, standing atop a steep and barren cliff, scarifying her body with her fingernails, throwing off chunks of flesh, sprays of blood, locks of hair, her teeth, her nails; and wherever one of them fell, quickly and instantaneously, life ended.

Men, by the thousands, slumped over and fell in tragic silence like tall grass plucked from a lush field; trees withered; crystal clear water from fresh streams blackened in stagnation; birds tucked their wings and tumbled dead out of the air.

Finally, in an assault by the specter, the sky became bloodied in clumps, and soon the bright stars went out.

Then the skeleton began to move wildly, waggling and leaping; it hurled itself off the cliff onto the heap of corpses and, trampling it in triumph, danced and swelled dramatically, filling the entire space until there was nothing left but the ossuary, overtaking the heavens and earth, and, at its very top, where its ribs were like an enormous rainbow, was the monstruous, putrid skull, with two opaque eyes rolling in their sockets like dead stars—corpses of the sun and the moon, oscillating and still glowing in their final stirrings.

I awoke in anguish, drenched in the sweat of torment, and jumping out of my bed, I stood in the middle of the room, frightened and anxious, while the hideous, pungent odor continued to hover, making the air so thick it tingled.

The night shadows were already beginning to fade into the bright colors of dawn. I went out to my sitting room, and feeling the healthy breeze of morning on my face, I greedily took in huge gulps of air, as if I'd emerged on the surface of the sea after a protracted, asphyxiating dive.

I leaned out the window, enjoying the marvelous apotheosis of daybreak.

The sky, with its various shades of daylight, from gentle purple to embellished gold, its glowing visage resplendent as if an immense curtain of fire were slowly rising, was superimposing itself over the soft, fading blue.

The trees swayed in voluptuous movement, rustling their branches and seeming to flamboyantly pose themselves to receive the sun. The leaves, in the soft light that spread a golden glow, flattened with greedy eagerness.

From every twig among the top branches, swift birds took wing amid chirps and cheerful trills, their flights intersecting in an aerial festival, as the clear skies warmed with the triumphantly rising sun.

I went downstairs to the bath, and in an effort to conjure up funereal impressions, I decided to work all day, opening wide the doors of the "dream" I had there at hand, taking refuge in it as among the flowering trees of an enchanted forest.

And I had just sat down in front of James's manuscript when the first ray of sunlight streaked through the open window.

VI

Poets do not lie when they say that supernatural beings covet the contingent life of the ephemerals.

The undine,[31] *in the shadows of the afternoon, rises to the water's surface and tumbles onto the floating lily, awaiting the traveler. If she spies one, be he a graceful nobleman or a poor, ragged shepherd, she will praise him, throbbing with the beat of desire, puffing out her chest, twinkling her green eyes, her pale cheeks suffused with pink. When she sees him up close, she will leap agilely onto the stepping stones, bouncing lightly among the dense branches, bursting lithely into the meadow, and stand and curve her torso impressively as she pushes back her dripping hair and displays her fully naked self, inviting him in a languid voice, and seducing him with lascivious gestures. And if she takes him by the hand, she embraces him with desperation, wrapping herself voluptuously around him as she glues her cold lips onto his mouth and kisses the life out of him.*

---

31. An *undine* is an elemental being that inhabits water (a water nymph).

Is it because she lacks lovers in her crystalline retreat that she leaves, in search of them on earth? Let the answer come from the village maidens, for they don't risk going to the river after the welcoming call so as not to be betrayed by the male undine that crouches in the grass on the wet riverbank.

Fairies, whose status is respected by all of nature, reluctantly flee from the love of water sprites. They watch them in the cold moonlight, wandering wildly in the mist, dancing in circles around the lakes, singing and playing simple instruments.

They desire the ardent loves of earth and use sorcery to attract the mortals, seeking in them what they do not find in the sylphs and elves, the desire that enervates them, the sister desire of death, more violent than the cold and infertile love of the immortals.

The opposite is always preferred—desire is the free and capricious bird that flies toward contrast.

How many times, looking down from the top of the splendid tower, surrounded by all worldly pleasures, have I envied the sad fate of the shepherd boy passing through the valley, huddled in his threadbare cloak, trampling through the snow on the rough path leading to the farm or the ramshackle, unlit shed?

Accustomed to wonder, I was no longer surprised by the most extraordinary occurrences of my life in captivity.

To see, as I did, in the fading twilight, the immense shadow of a bird whose feathers were shining; see it swoop down into the recess around the pointed arch, setting it ablaze with its flaming crest, scraping the panes with its golden talons and spectacularly shattering it, leaving only a trace of fire in its place, was to me a spectacle as commonplace as the gushing of gargoyles on a rainy day. I was more entertained and fascinated by the slow flight of the wild ducks that rose out of the lakes in bands and disappeared behind the hills, appearing for a moment as black specks against the flame-colored background of sunset.

What were those wonders for someone who lived them, if my days and nights were always a continuous miracle?

So, my first impression, as I went from the chamber to the ballroom, whose wide-open windows let in pure fresh air, receiving the joyful sunshine and the fragrance of flowering meadows, delighting my eyes as they contemplated the blue sky, superimposed in relief against the contours of the mountains, was simply one of pleasure. But then, however, remembering the harsh winter's day before, a night of wind and snow, and recalling the hideous apparition that had taken hold of me, I shuddered.

How had the thick snow melted so quickly? How had the gusty winds subsided into gentle breezes? How had the parched groves that out there had fallen into a coma become lush and florid? How, during a single dream, did heaven and earth go from sterile winter to the beauty and vigor of spring?

I looked out, confused, when I heard footsteps and immediately felt the cherished scent of Maya. I turned around. It was her. She was smiling, beautiful, with a rose on her bosom and a bunch of yellow carnations gracefully placed at her waist. I asked her about the change that had occurred so quickly, and she calmly responded:

"If there was any miracle, it was your three-month slumber. You fell asleep when the crows were still scraping the snow. Then came the first swallows, and they found you sleeping. Neither the call of the lark nor the trilling of the nightingales in the low-lying land roused you from the lethargy you had fallen into. Fields and knolls turned green, trees and hedges were covered with flowers, and, with festive haste, the pristine streams you had left behind drifted lightly. Swarms of bees invaded your chambers, colorful butterflies fluttered around your bed . . . and you slept. For three long months, you slept."

"And why did my slumber last so long?"

"Because you discovered the face of death." These words pronounced in a mysterious tone left me puzzled, and the entire scene of the night before flowed through my

memory, every detail included—the fearful pilgrimage through the dazzling rooms, the mournful and frightening spectacle of the coffin, the corpse of Arhat, the apparition at the entrance to my chamber.

Terrified, feeling a piercing chill as if an iron had penetrated my chest, motionless and nearly speechless, I asked about the extraordinary man.

"He is waiting for you," said the maiden, gazing at me sadly, her eyes misting. "Come with me and say farewell to everything around you and to me who loves you because you will never again see what you are leaving behind. Your cocoon will open to free the butterfly. You will understand everything you have longed for. Come!" And without another word, she moved quickly ahead, through the door, into the hall, and down the long, winding staircase, with me following . . .

Below, in the courtyard of the idols, she stopped, held her cold hand out to me, and her beautiful eyes—which still light up my soul like the dead stars that shine in the depth of the sky—appeared to dissolve into tears.

For a moment, our clasped hands pressed together more tightly, and we stared at each other in silence, but a figure appeared out of the ivy that covered the pointed arch of the stone and bronze gateway, and in it I recognized Arhat, whose hand held a long stem on which hung a lily of incomparable whiteness.

I trembled. At the imperative nod from the domineering man, I freed my cold, shaking hands from Maya and obediently followed in the direction of the dignitary.

Side by side we walked.

Sunlight blazed over the park, flourishing in every aspect. Fragrances rose in gentle exhalation, impregnating the air.

Vain peacocks, their shimmering tails open in shining fans, stood motionless on the banks of the lake where graceful white swans, slowly treading the water, calmly glided by as if carried on a breeze.

Pheasants flew from branch to branch with a flash of iridescent feathers; and here, there, and everywhere, intersecting in flight, were birds with sparkling, variegated plumage; butterflies; bees; and all the winged creatures, basking in the light under the glowing dust of the sun as in a fiery baptism of fecundity.

Arhat, preoccupied, walked as he gazed around in rapture. Now and then, he took long, greedy gulps of the lily.

Although we followed a sandy path on which my footsteps crackled, the master's steps made no sound, and at one point, as we stood shoulder to shoulder, I felt not his body but a soft, pleasant heat like a ray of sunlight upon me. There was only a single shadow in front of me, blackening the dirt; on Arhat's side, preceding him, a brightness shone, and around him the leaves gave off a mysterious glow.

We slowly crossed a secluded pathway of glistening gravel and reached a clearing where the delicate grass was spread in a carpet so soft that walking over it was pure delight.

Not infrequently through the branches would be two large eyes, wet and sweet, spying on us—some antelope or doe.

The twigs rustled in gentle movement with the breeze, and a pungent, wild smell filled the air like the aromatic breath of healthy trees.

Not a soul besides the animals was around to enjoy the glory of that dazzling morning in the beauty of the park, whose appearance changed as we moved along, leaving on either side dark depths of woods or wide-open expanses, mirror-like lakes or waves of bubbling water that formed falls over rough stones and overgrowth, a shed or a grotto, thickets or smooth mounds of soft grass under the shade of flowers, where just a glance revealed the work and careful tending of man.

Herds of deer flocked to the hedges, leaping and often colliding over the footpaths, and there was a fluttering of wings in hasty departures, a twitter of alarmed birds, flights of insects, the rustle of fields under the slithering of lizards, and, at a distance, in the shade of a huge oak tree, deer grazed, and one in the front, his head held high, gazed hostilely out as if watching our steps, ready to protect the tribe, of which he appeared to be the powerful chief.

But Arhat continued on, and I, in no mood to speak, followed behind, uneasy, if not fearful and imagining absurdities.

As we approached a gurgling fountain, hidden among delicate plants drenched from the continuous flow of water, he stared quietly at the ground, his head suspended in thought.

After a second, he turned to face me, beckoning for me to sit on one rock while he sat on another, and after breathing in the scent of the lily, he said:

"One afternoon—I was living near London at the time—it was the onset of winter, when night fell early—I was studying alone when, from out on the street, I heard loud voices, terrified cries, and frightened screams. I ran to the window and, as I opened it, saw in the black sludge, beginning to gush with blood, two twisted bodies. A wagon was speeding away, amid a public outcry, and since it was closing time at the factories and workshops, a large crowd had quickly gathered at the site of the accident.

"At the time, I had as my companion a Tibetan colossus who served me with dedication and respect. I called him over and, pointing to the corpses, ordered him to

bring them to me. I do not know how he did it, but it took him no time at all.

"I carried the mortal remains back to my study, and after examining them carefully, I recognized that one was the body of a boy whose head was now nothing more than shapeless pulp; the other, a girl, had a crushed chest that was a mass of flesh and shards of bone, bleeding profusely.

"Availing myself of the notions of the arcane arts,[32] *since I was still able to find traces, or better still, manifestations of the presence of the seven principles, I retained the jiva, or life force, causing it to attract the rest that circulated in an aura around the flesh, and with pressing urgency, I removed from the bodies what had not been affected. Taking the head of the girl and fitting it onto the body of the boy, I reestablished circulation, revived the fluids, and thus retaining the principles from atma,*[33] *which is the divine essence itself, I remade a life in a human body, in a man's body, which is you."*

Such a strange revelation made in so composed a manner, with the simplicity of natural conversation, shook me in such a way that I felt drained and blinded,

---

32. The arcane arts broadly include knowledge of a number of beliefs and practices, such as mysticism, yogic practices, theosophy, miracles, mesmerism, and white or black magic (Sahoo).

33. In theosophy, *atma* is the supreme universal self, the seventh principle of cosmos, and, correspondingly, the divine aspect in man's constitution ("Theosophical Terms").

but my breath was restored by a delicate aroma that sweetly pervaded me. When I reopened my eyes, here is what I saw: Arhat was beside me, holding over my face the lily whose fragrance had so delighted me.

"Listen," he continued, "I will not tell you the mystery since it is written. Here it is." He bent down and, brushing aside the leafy branches that adorned the fountain, picked up a silver-plated cedar box, opened it, and pulled out a book, which he handed me.

"I had intended to give you the knowledge of what is described in this volume, which is your bible, but you hastened my travel with your curiosity. I had to return in the 'aura' from the beyond to reach the body, which was still mine and which you profaned with your imprudent look.

"Your punishment was benign: three months in the prisons of death, but what you lost is inestimable. You have benefited me by speeding up the hours of the great and definitive renunciation.

"Before the sun reaches its zenith, I will have freed myself from this step of anguish, becoming part of the atma. The body being Earth, what is life if not the prison in which we die? You shortened the time to my ascension.

"Life is a sequence of activity and inertia, a necklace of interspersed dark and light beads, days and nights. Each night that slips away takes you to a new morning. Rein-

carnations are great days on which we purify ourselves, passing from one to another through the shadow of death, which is night, at the end of which shines the daybreak. The never-ending day, light at its fullest, clear, calm, and infinite, will not dawn until the cycle of corporeal, material existence is complete—when purity through atonement becomes equal to that of the beginning—when the pureness of old age is equal to the innocence of the cradle.

"From sleep, you proceed to the morning with memory, which is the consciousness of the past; death, which is a longer sleep, erases that vestige of life, so that in reincarnations there are vague recollections, but there can be no certainty: scars persist but memories fade away."

He breathed in the lily at length before continuing: "My banishment is close at hand, so I must be brief and as clear as words permit. Your whole life is in this book, but the ideogram in which it was written can only be deciphered by someone who has achieved perfection.

"If you succeed in discovering a superior intellect that can interpret the symbols, the world will consider you an angel among men, a master of all mercies, of all prestige, a sovereign will in an amazing spirit; if, however, you do not obtain the key to the arcane, woe is you."

He turned his sharp eyes in my direction and gazed at me for a long time. Motionless, only the lily swung like a pendulum in his hand.

After a moment he continued: "On the same night I was able to conjoin the two bodies, which belonged to death and which I restored to life, ceding to the earth the tribute it was due, as the pieces were buried by my faithful servant. I left home to come to this old castle where, at the cost of my own existence and at the expense of my own energy, I nourished the life you have today, giving you my fluid with the same loving indifference as the mother bird who claws into her breast and pecks at the wound with her beak to obtain the blood she uses to feed the nest.

"You are truly the child of my soul.

"But no sooner was life established in you when I began to be assailed by an irrepressible desire to know which soul should influence your life, imparting its moral character.

"Two wandered around the wreckage of the flesh, according to the power of karma, which is the force of integration. Only one, however, needed to prevail since only one of the two independent lives could survive. As soon as signs of action of the seven principles affecting matter were manifested in the remade body, the existence of a soul was clearly proven. Which one would be victorious—that of the boy or that of the girl?

"All my attempts to solve this mystery failed. I lay awake long nights, lost endless and consecutive days bent

over your cradle, casting inculcations in vain. My senses were sharpened for naught, for what could I obtain from the psychic inertia of an infant?

"Dorka, who accompanied you from your first hours, always attentive, with the solicitude of a priestess at the voice of the oracle, died in uncertainty without getting even the slightest hint of suspicion.

"I insisted on exposing you to the two sexes, looking for the most perfect specimens of beauty and grace, of flexibility and integrity, of tenderness and dignity, of fragile innocence that surrenders itself and towering strength that dominates: Siva and Maya. Seeing them convinced me that the soul accompanying you, whichever it was, would reveal its nature by inclination through proximity.

"It oscillated in ephemeral affection on whims more of sensibility than of love. You never showed any predilection, and the flesh remained impassive in the presence of one or the other, even if your gaze at times was merely moved in admiration, delighting in the beauty with the same enchantment felt when drinking in the scenery or the bright colors of the sky at dawn and dusk.

"Your face increasingly emphasized feminine beauty, but your body became robust in masculine vigor, and your heart always remained mute, inert, and indifferent in equal measure between the two sexes that were paired to dispute it.

"Perhaps your being is only now emerging. You have entered puberty, which is the season in which the soul opens itself up, revealing its loving nature, igniting the fires of sensuality in the flesh.

"If the feminine prevails in you, reflected in the beauty of your face, the face of your sister, you will be a monster; if the masculine spirit triumphs, as the strength of your muscles would have us believe, you will be like a magnet for lust. But wretched will you be, since there has never been another like you in the world, if the two souls hovering over the reborn flesh have succeeded in insinuating themselves into it.

"The Linga Sharira,[34] *or astral body, the ambient 'aura' that circulates in a halo around your head, is the final principle that abandons the body, and your head is feminine. Is your heart then masculine?*

"Unfortunate will you be if the two principles have managed to penetrate your being—discord will accompany you like a shadow accompanies your body. In loving, you will be jealous and disgusted at yourself. You will be an incoherent anomaly, wanting with your heart and loathing with your head, and vice versa. Your right

---

34. In theosophy, *Linga Sharira* is defined as the "'Astral Body' of man or animal; the vital and prototypal body; the reflection of the man of flesh. It is born before and dies or fades out, with the disappearance of the last atom of the body" ("Theosophical Terms").

hand will declare war on your left, one of your cheeks will burn with shame and disgust, while the other will glow in the modesty that is the emergence of desire. You will live between two fierce enemies.

"Woe is you . . . ! Tell me: Where does your heart take you? What do your senses require? Where do your dreamy eyes linger with more enchantment?"

He looked at me quizzically, and since he'd heard not a word from my terrified silence, he shuddered, and lightning flashed in the sky.

"It's late!" he finally sighed, saying wistfully, "The lily is starting to wither and droop. Life is fading away!

"Just as the bird needs a branch on which to stand, I needed a body that could support me. I chose the flower, and flowers die."

Sure enough, the lily went limp, curving over its stem, soft, yellowing, and Arhat, as if to take advantage of the final seconds, hastily spoke these words in a punishing tone:

"Farewell! I have told you all of this so you will not suffer. It is enough to have to suffer from what you carry inside. You will find someone who can guide you on your first steps outside your paradise. The fortune I bequeathed you will ensure the pleasures of life and the servility of men. You will see them bow before you like a field of wheat in the wind, and you will march past, trampling

upon preconceptions and conventions, honor, love, justice and laws, strength and pride, innocence and misery, and, far from crying out against reproach, the nobles, the honest folk, those who are pure at heart, the outraged spouses, the disgraced virgins, the judges, the patriots reduced to infamy by your bribery, will welcome the affront and proclaim your virtue, the more you bury them in the quagmire of gold.

"Vile gold! Do with it what the sun does to a flame: light, clarity, warmth, life. Gold from the mine is the true fire of this cursed land. Make it your sun, your heavenly light, using it for the good. Be good.

"A coin is the wheel that leads to all infamy and to salvation: placed on the edge of the abyss, it plummets; thrown into the sky, it is a star. Be good.

"Go and search this vast land for someone who will give you the key to the secret enclosed in the mystical book. Now follow me. I want to leave you where it is easy for your guide to find you."

He got up and took the lead, and I saw that as he drew further away, with him went the light that illuminated the forest, where shadows and the cold of winter afternoons fell.

Light moved along with the man as if it radiated from him, and as we passed a flowering acacia tree, its branches began to sway, causing the tree to sprinkle the abundance of its corymbs, and the flowers, falling on the master, imparted a shower of gold over his body, causing the butterflies, bees, and everything else to sparkle like pollen from the air when caught in the path of a sunbeam.

His body was no longer an obstacle to the view of the landscape through which I saw everything as if through a golden stained-glass window. Branches were lit by the glow of his chest, his feet were two bright spots that made the gravel sparkle, his hands refracted iridescent rays, brightening the bushes over which they hovered.

Diaphanous and luminous was the light, and as it approached me, it gave off only a soft sensation of warmth. Now and again, it blended with me, or I would step into it and feel as if I were in bright sunshine, and my shadow would disappear into the ground.

The lily was withering. Arhat, taciturn, seemed to float on air—his feet together, motionless, did not even touch the ground, and straight, unbending, his head dazzling and erect, he followed beside me like an ethereal being that had freed itself of what was human in him, acquired from humanity, shedding from his staring eyes thick tears, shining like diamonds that rolled down his magnificent cheeks onto the ground or the grass, where they continued to shine.

We reached a clearing. Arhat made a flickering gesture with his straight arm, indicating to me a twisted path, which I followed, bowing as if to a threat.

A few steps on, I shivered, hearing a long, drawn-out sigh. A strange force overtook me: I turned around and, amazed and awestruck, saw the luminous figure of the master as he rose in a slow ascent and faded away, vanishing little by little—only a translucent shimmer hovered, like the exhalation of roasted earth in summer, evaporating and rarifying until he disappeared completely. The lily alone remained swaying in the air. Suddenly, like a wounded bird, it fell, crumbling into pieces as it hit the ground.

In an instant, trills and the chatter of birdsong poured out in concert, deer roared passionately among the shady oaks, and the air became incredibly fragrant.

As for me, it was as if I had been blinded, gagged, and restrained. I plunged, breathless and paralyzed, into sudden darkness, rattled by a gloomy howling, as if a shell had been fitted to my ear or I lay imprisoned in the echoing and sinister tunnels of a catacomb. What happened? I don't know.

When I came to, I was in a carriage, traveling along a smooth white road between flowering hedges and cottages nestled in the shade of trees.

The mild afternoon was full of fragrance; and in the still air, now and then, a church bell rang. Swallows fluttered about, and under an azure mist the fields fell asleep.

Across from me, motionless and solemn, sat a blond man with thin side-whiskers, who held on his lap a box containing what I immediately recognized as the book of my destiny.

The words of Arhat came to me quickly, as if they were fresh on my mind, awaiting my recall: "I want to leave you where it is easy for your guide to find you."

So this was the man who was to introduce me to the world that to me already seemed complicated and hostile.

As if in response to my questioning gaze, he bowed his head slightly and murmured, "Sullivan." That was his name, and then, as if to relieve himself of the uncomfortable weight, he took from his pocket a black leather wallet and handed it to me, explaining, "About the Bank of England." Millions, Arhat's fortune.

And we exchanged not a single word until we reached London that night.

We disembarked at the Ambassador Hotel, where they were already waiting for us with the most spacious and sumptuously appointed rooms. And so began my real life.

When, in my calmest and most wistful of silences, I compared it with what I had forever left behind, it appeared even more wonderful and extraordinary.

My days spent in the lost manor house had flowed idly with the monotony of water flowing in clear rivers, gorgeous but always and invariably serene, with the same whining babble, the same snow-white flowers floating with the current, the same green branches reflected on the smooth surface, and in the whirlpool into which I had thrown myself, every minute brought surprises.

The first four days of my new life were, dare I say, fuller than the eighteen quiet ones I had spent lying around the melancholy manor house of the dreary valley.

Sullivan showed me everything: the most impressive luxury and the most moving and sordid misery.

I saw processions of princes and lines of galley slaves, some in arms. I heard choirs in cathedrals as vast as cities, and I heard the panting of ferrymen crossing the river and the mournful chants of laborers in their workshops. I heard the clank of gold and iron. I traversed the city and all its entrails—above ground, where I could see the sky, or underground, with a vaulted tomb weighing heavily on my chest. And I saw, with true amazement and shocked compassion, the machine, conqueror of man, the machine, causer of misery, crushing the poor to make money for the rich; the machine that banishes effort much like gunpowder renders bravery useless.

Water, fire, the ethereal spark, all the pure forces came together for the crime, stealing bread from the poor, undressing them, taking their homes, throwing them out on the street as naked and destitute as the grim day they were born.

I visited factories and workshops and was moved by the inhuman devices that, like plows that turn and groove the earth to kill the humble weeds from which the seeds of bread can grow free of parasites, displace the weak to the benefit of the strong. I saw it all.

We left the opulent squares and wallowed in the squalid alleyways that crawled with frightful, spectral, poignant people: men, women, and children eagerly seizing filthy rags to cover their emaciated nudity, gathering in a mob around us as they stretched out their scrawny hands to beg, rushing at us menacingly or else groveling tearfully.

Hideous creatures, spilling out of the dark pubs, some filthy, trembling with fever, others, apoplectically purple, staggering in their drunkenness, hoarse in their depravity or bellowing curses; prepubescent girls in rags taking us by the arm with lewd cynicism—children who never knew innocence—puffing out their skeletal chests, winking their spiritless eyes coquettishly, and nibbling shamelessly on their purplish lips.

We fled the ragged mobs and soon emerged into the splendor of the city.

Such sights lingered in my soul, leaving a bitter taste. And so truly did I understand the supernatural.

The "natural" should be the happy life I lived with the master, served by all the marvelous forces of heaven and earth, my every desire fulfilled, comforted in my sorrows, sheltered from the cold, shielded from the sun, strong and healthy, and even in the bitterest of winters, seeing around me budding flowers and ripening fruit and listening delightedly to sweet birdsong. The natural stayed there with the marvels, the wonders enhanced by goodness.

The supernatural only then appeared to me in the shadow of the temples of God, at the crushing feet of unrelenting justice; it was that—a scale with two pans on opposite sides: one weighed down to elevate the other to happiness, to misery, tears, just tears. The supernatural was that.

Endless was the affluence of the hotel's huge ballroom, under the blinding glow of the lights, reflected in the large mirrors and shimmering against the marble among abundantly flowered tables with their shining dishes and sparkling crystal; men in formal attire with rose boutonnieres, women in plunging necklines daringly displaying cleavage and backs. A hidden orchestra played softly.

Sullivan, always impassive, was indifferent to the hustle and bustle that left me rattled and annoyed.

Outside at night, the boorishness grew louder over the incessant and cascading racket. At all hours, one heard the sound of corks popping over the din of voices and raucous laughter.

It was a time of abundant revelry—gold would dissolve into joy. And in the square, the carriages passed through lines of wretches begging for alms, running from purity to vice, or watching for the perfect moment to steal or commit robbery at gunpoint in the shadows.

We would barely finish our somber dinner when Sullivan would invite me to the "evening's entertainment." We would go to theaters, concert halls, colossal circuses, or erotic cafes. He would drag me along. At first I was dazzled by it all, but the wonder would dissolve into monotony like the dust the wind lifts from the street that for a second is suspended, shining golden in the sun, only to then fall to the ground.

I was drawn to the silence. Shyness and annoyance made me recoil and flee from the insulting looks of the curious, noting the appalling shamelessness in the malicious insistence with which men would stare at me, and the lascivious brazenness in the ecstasy of women who stared at my face with shock.

I saw the nightly orgies, how vice took every form: in the free licentiousness with which women and young men would couple, consumed with intoxication; the rampant gambling and then, in the silent darkness, the sloppy steps of unsteady figures sniffing around as they sifted through the rubbish so as to beat the dogs to the dregs.

Retreating to the hotel with my heart filled with sadness, I could not sleep and would lean over the balcony, contemplating the vast city, magnificent in its lights, whose misery surprised me in its hideousness and made me think about the horror of that ulcerated body, glowing under the shafts of light like immense carcasses of dead animals emanating the luminous cloud of the reckless flame.

Oh, the supernatural!

My worries would disappear whenever my eyes spied the strange book. Then, remembering the words of Arhat, I focused my attention on the symbols, trying to tease out their secrets, questioning them with desperate eagerness.

How many times did I fall asleep over those impenetrable pages!

One day, I decided to consult the most well-known scholars who claimed to know the occult sciences, and for months, I wandered through palaces and garrets with the impenetrable book, listening to notables and modest researchers, and everyone who saw it would only send me back to the horror in which I lived, making it even worse with their words that took away all hope.

Sullivan, despite his solemn manner and rigid appearance of austerity, delighted only in worldly pleasures, and every morning, even though I had no connections in the city, he would bring me voluminous correspondence, and

I would open the letters at random, read invitations to parties, complaints of misery, lewd proposals, requests from gold diggers, and my hands would come out of the paperwork wet with tears and stained by mud.

Sullivan would say not a word, but he smiled at the seductions that besieged me, and I felt the incentive with which he encouraged me toward the repugnant depravity.

One day, disgusted with the material man who had been attached to me for life, and burning more intensely with the eagerness to know my own destiny, I decided to venture out into the world, visiting all the seats of the ancient sciences where perhaps I could find the individual destined to provide me with the key to the arcane.

I dismissed my guide with a check from the Bank of England that assured him abundant means to distract himself in enjoyment, and I set off for the Orient. For two years, without a day of rest, I climbed rugged mountains and crossed thick forests, roaming from sea to sea all over Asia, visiting the dens of contemplatives, consulting wise men and penitents, leaving forests to enter sacred shrines. I steeped myself in ancient, wild Thessaly. I walked through the log huts of the land of snow; I slept in the pleasing oases of sandy Africa; I listened to the fortune-tellers and prophets; I talked to the mystics of the frozen North, where, in the paleness of icebergs through the bone-chilling white nights, diaphanous spirits abound, and I found in man only a superficial knowledge of life. And my soul? Woe is me!

It was in Stockholm that I suffered the misfortune of falling in love for the first time, and that love . . . that love could only be engendered in a female soul.

Thus . . . my sister is the victor in me.

Lovingly accepted into the bosom of a noble family, whose coat of arms dates back centuries, I found the two young representatives of this august house to be the best friends I had ever had.

They were twins, and they were beautiful! Love entered with me into the virginal heart of the maiden, but it was to the young man that I devoted my soul; the young man who had made me the confidant of his love.

My soul struggled in intense anguish if I did not feel him near, but when he appeared, I would erupt in a violent rage, hating him, detesting him, and despising myself with contempt, as if I had become polluted.

His secrets would sting me deeply, and every tender word that alluded to his affection wounded me like an arrow to the heart, and just the name of his betrothed was excruciating torture. Poor me!

Oh, my strong soul, my virile soul, where are you that you are not defending me?

I would flee from the sweet sibling couple, flee from the genuine love and tenderness, ashamed of my dreadfulness and unhappy in that forbidden love. And, secluding myself, I would open the book in distress, staring at the symbols to find in them the truth, whatever it was, the solution to the terrible problem of my soul or of the twinned souls that fight in the turbulent arena that is my miserable heart.

I left. Since then, my life has become unbearable. The suffering took care of the interpretation of the symbols: I know that I am a wretch, that as Arhat said, "Wretched will you be, since there has never been another like you in the world."

Every flower has its own perfume, and a life cannot obey two rhythms. Two souls at war, feeling differently, render useless the instinct that is the basis of attraction.

A monster, a monster that devours itself, that is what I am.

The book cannot say more—it is just this, and it is suffering.

Imagine a bird that when taking off from its nest feels its claws ensnared in braces of steel. Longing for and drawn to the sky, it flaps its wings until it dies of exhaustion. That is how I will end up in the void, flying captive, belonging not to the sky nor to the earth, not to the trees nor to the heavens, imprisoned in space and on the branch . . . The absurd, the contradiction, the inconceivable—that is who I am.

VII

The afternoon sluggishly waned, saturated with fragrance, already growing melancholy in the fading colors when, repulsed by the arduous task, I pushed my hunched-over body away from the desk, my mouth bitter from the smoke of countless cigarettes, my head in a daze, stupefied and throbbing in the echoing void.

Both mind and body were suffering from the relentless work. I leaned back limp against the chair, stretching out my legs, my head exhausted, and there I lingered a moment in forgotten rest, replaying the dream in which, from the morning's earliest hours, stopping only for a simple lunch eaten hastily in my room, to that violet and melancholy twilight, I'd worked delightedly to convert the flowery language of James's wondrous original into the pale and pitiful sentences of a shabby rendering.

I smoked distractedly on a cigarette as I listened to the chirping of swallows approaching the house, my eyes in rapt attention to the twinkling glimmer of a lone star that had timidly emerged, seeming vexed and confused about being the only one in the immense desert of sky, still warm from the sun, streaked with purple stains like the bloody sand of a coliseum.

I could hear the babbling of neighborhood children, and it was as sweet and pleasurable as the sigh of silks in the gentle rustle of the palm trees, puffed by the sea breeze.

Faint sounds flowed fleetingly, rippling lightly in the silence. Little by little they grew louder, at first indistinct like a murmur, then distinct as a melody, clear, in joyous vibrations, swelling or receding as if oscillating in space. They erupted in a roar, bursting suddenly in clangor, followed by a deafening blast of brass and a rumble of drums before quickly dying away, leaving, in the mystical afternoon air and the quiet tranquility of that isolated street, a martial echo like the parade of a triumphant army through the quiet simplicity of a peaceful village, cradled in the shade of groves and gently rocked by the silence of the hills.

It was a military band passing by on the streetcar to Botafogo.

I roused myself in a stretch, my arms lifted as I yawned disjointedly, and standing up, staggering in dozy footsteps, I walked to the window, where I leaned over in euphoric contemplation.

The palm trees looked like bronze, still shimmering in the last of the sun's glow. Pigeons traversed in tranquil flight, and the scent that rose from the soil, wet from watering, was fresh and pleasant like the breath of health.

The bell rang downstairs, calling us to dinner.

I lingered, not wishing to move, seized by that serenity, watching, with the curiosity of one before a new sight, the twinkling of the stars, the sun's bright colors fade, and the slow spread of shadows that grew darker and darker as more stars appeared.

Soon, humble voices awoke in the shallow grass—the evening song of the tiny residents of burrows, the crickets, that create a rhythm in the silence, like the monotonous ticktock of a watch in the pitch dark. And the fireflies quickened among the branches, carrying their wandering glows to all the dark corners.

The gardener scraped his scythe with a frightening ring as he softly sang.

Again the dinner bell rang.

I quickly freshened up and dressed half-heartedly, annoyed as if awakened from a bad night's sleep, and left the room that reeked of smoke, slowly descending the stairs, feeling each riser softly give way to my steps, malleable as rubber.

The boarders were beginning to gather in the already illuminated dining room, where white dishware was placed atop the smooth tablecloth decorated with fresh flowers that lent color and fragrance to the simple table.

The sound of voices drew me to the veranda, where a group stood arguing. The subject was a telegram, and Pericles, stoked by patriotism, his tie flapping, was ranting hyperbole as he reminisced about our epic history—brutal battles, feats of bravery, brazen acts—and used dramatic gestures to praise the toughness and humble bravery of the northern caboclos[35] and the unrestrained push of the southern cavalrymen, brave gauchos[36] whose spears, in indomitable attacks, defeated the fiercest troops, routing them in a screaming melee.[37] And red-faced, apoplectic, his veins turgid and purple, crumpling the newspaper in which the telegram had appeared, he threw it violently to the ground as if he were throwing a gauntlet at the feet of some despicable scoundrel in disgust.

---

35. In this context, a *caboclo* refers to a native of the Amazonian interior (northern Brazil).

36. In Portuguese, a *gaúcho* refers to a native of the Brazilian state of Rio Grande do Sul.

37. These lines likely refer to the nineteenth century, a period when several provinces sought to separate from the Portuguese Empire. Insurrections exploded across Brazil—the Cabanagem, the Farroupilha Revolution, the Sabinada Revolt, and the Balaiada. The 1800s ended with the War of Canudos, armed conflicts between the Brazilian army and residents of Canudos ("Brazil"; "War").

Everyone laughed at his gesture, causing him to grow even more furious, his eyes bulging with rage as he thumped his chest, offering it to the spears and gunfire of the scoundrels who dared insult the homeland.

"If there's a war, I'll drop everything and enlist. No, my patriotism is not just words . . ."

"It is of photographic plates," remarked Basílio snidely, his face quivering in laughter. Pericles choked, locking his flashing eyes on the bookkeeper, whose fat, puffy face was swollen with irony.

"Look, my friend. During the revolt, I spent many a night on the Cajú lines, with gun in hand.[38] I'm not one of those who runs off into the woods at the smell of gunpowder. I'm not about the prose. If there is a war . . . I will march!"

"Come on, now. Stop it," argued the Commander, angry. And rising up on his toes, he haughtily inquired, "War with whom? Why?"

"With whom? You're still asking?"

"Yes. With whom?" Pericles took a step back and dramatically pointed his finger at the balled-up newspaper at

---

38. Given that Basílio is one of the older boarders in the novel, this likely refers to the Brazilian naval revolts, armed mutinies promoted mainly by Admirals Custódio José de Melo and Saldanha da Gama and their fleet of rebel Brazilian navy ships against what was claimed to be unconstitutional: President Floriano Peixoto (1891–94) staying in power.

the bottom of the stairs: "Read the telegram. It's down there!"

"What telegram, what nonsense. It's just a scam, politics, a bargaining chip. What this country needs are arms, arms that can work the land, to take advantage of the uncultivated wealth out there. Enough of your bravado, my friend."

"Bravado?" he said, as he curled his pale lips in anger. "If you were Brazilian . . ."

The Commander shot the entrepreneur a terrible look, his arms stiffening and his fingers bending as if retracting from pain, and taking a step forward, his lips shaking in anger, bellowed, "No, I'm not Brazilian, but I love this country much more than you, sir, who want to bloody it and crush it," and burning with anger, he roared, "Give it to the English!" The other man recoiled, stunned. "Yes, sir . . . to the English! I have here everything that is mine, my fortune and my life. Everything, do you understand, Mr. Pericles? Everything! And you?" He held back in defiance, his eyes fixed on the panic-stricken face of the entrepreneur. He rubbed his hand over his shiny bald head and for another moment cocked his eyes at the livid face of the patriot, breathing anxiously, and bending his torso, supercilious and hostile, his lips quivering in a burst of rage—the violence of a decisive insult was felt. Finally, he said, "Do you know what else, my friend?" There was an uncomfortable silence among the group, and the Commander finished: "Let's go in for the soup that's better before it gets cold."

It was a relief to all, and Basílio, to sound the final note with a joke, enjoined, "To the table!" and everyone went into the dining room laughing.

Fortunately for the entrepreneur, subdued from the humiliation of the assault by the Commander, Brandt appeared with the ever-loquacious Décio, still in the doorway, dressed as a dandy in light flannel, asking Miss Barkley for permission to offer her a bouquet of red carnations that he had brought from Petrópolis, a cluster of which he wore in his buttonhole.

The noisy entrance of the student brightened the mood, and the Englishwoman, always taciturn, crumpled her emaciated face, revealing her teeth, large and yellow as beans, as she drew her pale lips into a smile.

"I'm here to ask the Miss to forgive me for my ungrateful absence. The end of the year is coming fast, and I need to steal a few hours from sweet love and tender friendship to devote to those suffering from illnesses, to the human pain that will guarantee my bright future." He sat down, opened his napkin, and, offering a grateful glance as the servant served the soup before murmuring to him in affable kindness, said, "Everything is good around here. This is the house of Hygia,[39] the temple of good health."

Basílio grumbled: "A barracks, sir. We're being threatened to go out into the field with weapons. Our friend Pericles is going to enlist in the army, and we're joining him in solidarity."

The Commander chewed his roast, and the entrepreneur, again assuming his proud carriage, used his napkin to wipe his lips, and, after thoroughly chewing his mouthful, exclaimed, "It's true!"

"Enlist? You, sir?"

"And why not?" And, warming up: "Me and all the true patriots." He straightened up with arrogance and banged his silverware down on the table. Facing the student, he asked, "Tell me, you who are young, courageous, and enthusiastic. In the event of a war with a foreign country, will you stay, or will you go?"

Décio replied, sighing meekly, "Stay."

"You?" Pericles answered firmly, "You wouldn't stay!"

"I wouldn't stay?"

"You wouldn't stay! You'd march. You'd be one of the first."

39. Hygia is the goddess of health in Greek mythology. Décio refers here to the recently fumigated boardinghouse.

"According to the Gospel," and he explained, "My patriotism is not bellicose, my dear Mr. Pericles. I don't have the Camonian arm.[40] Besides, the wars this century are tremendously lethal, bolstered by terrible devices. Thus, it's necessary for one man to remain in the homeland to serve as a seed to repopulate it and write, in eternal pages, the superb epic of its greatest heroes. I will be that chosen man. While my compatriots win—because I do not admit the possibility of defeat—I, in the deserted silence of the motherland, will compose the perfect alexandrines that for centuries to come will carry the heroes' fame along with their names. And on the day the troops return, I will go to the Hotel Pharoux[41] with a great lyre and, naked, crowned with laurels, like Sophocles before the Greeks of Salamina,[42] will cross the avenue, leading the armies and singing a victory hymn." But suddenly, he pushed himself up, saying bitterly, "But you, sir, my friend Pericles, who bears the name of the great Grecian

---

40. Luís Vaz de Camões (1524–80) is considered Portugal's greatest poet. He wrote a considerable amount of lyric poetry and drama but is best remembered for his epic work *Os Lusíadas* (*The Luciads*), which describes Vasco da Gama's discovery of the sea route to India.

41. Rio de Janeiro's first hotel (1816–1959), located near Praça XV (then called Largo do Paço), built by the French-born Louis Pharoux shortly after the Portuguese court arrived in Rio.

42. Sophocles (496–406 BCE) was one of classical Athens's great tragic playwrights. In 480 BCE he was chosen to lead the paean (a choral chant to a god) celebrating the Greek victory over the Persians at the Battle of Salamis ("Sophocles").

who made Athens the capital of beauty,[43] have no right to think about wars."

"I agree!" growled the Commander, busying himself with his pudding.

"War is the motivation of tyrants, the strength of barbarians. Intelligent men and superior nations win with clear judgement, and if swords are rattled, it is the law that strikes out the rotten, like a scalpel in the hands of a surgeon. Let's not talk of war. Let's talk of love and beauty, beauty that is the wonder of life."

"And if we are insulted?"

"No one is insulting us."

"Oh, no one is insulting us?"

"No one," said the student, sternly.

"Have you not read the newspaper?"

"No, my friend, I haven't, nor do I intend to. My newspaper is the blue one overhead. In it I read the days and nights, the beautiful articles on clarity and shadow that are the golden clouds and the shining stars. The rotating machinery that interests me is the world. And talking about beauty: How is the British Apollo? The beautiful James, marvel and wonder of the city?"

---

43. Pericles (495–429 BCE) was an Athenian statesman who was influential in the development of both Athenian democracy and the Athenian empire in the late fifth century BCE.

"He tucked himself away in Tijuca, chasing butterflies," said the Commander.

"He hasn't been around here?"

"No."

"Strange man!" Basílio smiled slyly, lowering his head to his plate.

Miss Barkley said, "I think he's getting ready to leave."

"Leave us?"

"Yes. He's going back to England."

"Why?"

"He's an odd one."

The Commander nodded, "Crazy! Crazy is what he is, and mad."

"Why crazy, Commander?" asked Décio.

"Why? Would a reasonable man do the things he does? You only know him from seeing him. Ask your friend there who lives in the room next to him.

Décio looked at me with questioning eyes, and I answered:

"The Commander is mistaken. Mister James is an excellent neighbor. I have no reason to complain."

"Well, I'm sorry I can't say the same, and I assure you that if he stayed another month in this house, I'd be the one moving because I'm no fall guy. The son of a gun never sleeps, walking around upstairs all night. I'll be damned! Go with God. Handsome he is . . . but insufferable!"

"Well," said the student, "I would give years of my life to spend a day with him. He's a fellow that interests me, a stranger. He must have quite a unique story." He added, "Commander, beauty like that in a man . . . there's a mystery there! Happy is the one who can figure it out!"

Basílio, always sarcastic, lifting his napkin to his face, wickedly repeated the student's comment into the bristly ear of the Commander, who snickered. But Brandt, who up until then had remained aloof, eating slowly with eyes downcast, put his silverware down and, steadying himself in a purposeful manner, turned to face the bookkeeper, whose smile was gradually fading, as if hiding away in the refuge of his fat cheeks.

They stared at each other, but the artist got the upper hand, causing the other to grow pale and lower his gaze, and the entire table saw what was happening even though many were unaware since they had not noticed the wicked whispering of the know-it-all Commander.

When we got up, the sullen Brandt, hands in his pockets, walked right out onto the veranda with an air of disgust and, not waiting for coffee, disappeared into the garden.

Décio, who held me by the arm, had grabbed me to talk about his love, an obligatory subject in all his conversations.

He extolled the divine woman, muse and goddess-like inspirer of all his verses, but she always reminded him of death, holding him to her love with a tightfisted and inescapable greed with which the grave takes possession of the corpse. She surrendered herself in abandon in his arms, with the passive fatigue of a victim aspiring to martyrdom, the scandal of a surprise that would expose her to her husband's vengeance, casting her, bloody and naked, out to the curious eyes of the world and its mire of gossip. She was a remarkable woman, romantic to the point of insanity. "Sometimes, sweetly pushing me away, she weeps in silence, but she is even more beautiful covered in tears. If I question her, she responds in a voice that moves and arouses me: 'I'm afraid.' And once, she described her fear reflected in a dream: 'We were surprised. I saw him come in with a gun, heard the crack of the gun, felt the pain of the wounds, the flowing heat of blood, I struggled and died. Once dead, however, I read the newspaper reports describing our love and lamenting your talent, taken so soon from the world of letters, and my beautiful youth cut short so tragically. And I saw us both, side by side, cold and rigid among the mercy candles, on the morgue table, a jeering crowd around us, and I still loved you, my heart, spiritless and cold, still asked for yours, my crusty mouth still thirsted for your kisses, my shrouded body still yearned for your body.

How awful!' And do you know what? That obsession is beginning to take hold of me." And in a voice heavy with sadness and longing, he said, "It's inevitable, my friend. I leave home every night with the certainty that I'm going to die, and when I'm holding that woman close, inhaling her breath, there are times when I shudder, overtaken by a stabbing pain like a dagger piercing my heart. And I kiss her, I kiss her lips, her eyes, her hair, relinquishing my soul to her, my entire life. What madness! I'm lost and cannot escape, I can't. That love is my fate. It's stupid. Let's go."

He glanced around. "And Brandt? One day, that one's going to blow up at the bookkeeper. That fellow is annoyingly unpleasant and bad-mouthed to the point of slander. It's irritating. He's like a snake. Brandt is right. Let's go calm him down. He left in a rage!"

The piano offered a sweet prelude, and the light, filtering through the window of the cottage, gilded the shining branches of the flowering jasmine tree.

We walked along, and as we crossed the grove of softly scented acacia trees, I stopped the student with an urgent and overriding need to share my secret, to convey to a resourceful spirit the marvelous secret James Marian had left with me.

"You said, speaking of James, that there must be a mystery in his life . . ."

"Yes, a divine mystery. I said it then and say it again because I feel it is the case."

"And you're right, Décio."

The student looked at me up and down. "Do you know something?"

"I know that he's a poet."

"Yes, the essence of Apollo."

"Or a madman."

"What?"

"If he's not in fact a prodigy in the occult sciences."

"I don't understand you, man. You're speaking a hieratic language; you sound like an initiate proclaiming wonders."

"Do you have anything to do?"

"If you promise to explain your abstruse words, I tell you that even if I were entrusted with the task of shepherding the stars, the wolf Fenrir[44] could devour them without me even stepping foot in front of him because I would rather listen to you, sacrificing even my love, and I offer you the hours of this night, which promises to be stupendous. Tell me!"

And, whirling on his heels, inhaling great gulps of air, he gushed in delight: "How beautiful the magnolias

---

44. Fenrir is a wolf in Norse mythology and one of the children of Loki and the giantess Angrboða.

smell! Fleshy flowers, virgin breasts. Can you smell them? But, please, tell me what you know."

Taking him by the arm and walking slowly up and down the grove of acacia trees, I briefly summarized the story of James's beginning and the mysterious book, still forbidden to all minds.

Décio listened to me with an incredulous smile, and when I finished speaking, he began to laugh so hard that I could not help but smile.

"You have mounted Pegasus, the allerion[45] of dreams. You wrote a novel and want to attribute it to the misanthrope. It's a well-known process. Go, go get the original, man of fantasy, while I prepare the mind of the maestro, who is like the furious Ajax,[46] to listen to you and enjoy."

"I assure you, on my word, it is true. I'll bring the original to convince you."

"Yes, man. Go quickly. It's a beautiful night. We'll welcome the dawn to the sound of your phrases, and the blond goddess with the rosy cheeks will be proud of you. Go!" And, laughing, he continued on to the cottage, humming a popular tune.

---

45. An *allerion* is an eagle depicted in coats of arms with expanded wings but no beak or feet.

46. Ajax is a Greek mythological hero, the son of King Telamon and Periboea and half brother of Teucer, renowned for his size, strength, and great courage.

The house seemed deserted. The cold night had forced the boarders to retire. Through the lighted window of the basement, a slender shadow came and went: no doubt Crispim was memorizing texts. In the dining room, a gas nozzle stood guard in the darkness.

I went upstairs to my quarters and, as the room was brightening, began to gather up the papers. I picked up the mysterious volume and was about to leave when I heard a light knock on the door.

Thinking it was Alfredo, who often appeared at night to check on the bedroom arrangements, a pretext that provided him opportunities for numerous small gratuities, I said, without turning around, "Come in."

The door creaked slowly open, and I heard the sound of footsteps and then silence. I turned around and was surprised to see James Marian standing in front of me.

I stepped forward to speak to him, with sincere joyful excitement, but was met with cold diffidence. I offered him my desk chair, stunned.

The Englishman looked like marble—his eyes still, without the slightest flicker of his white, impassive face, motionless and stiff, his hand resting on the back of the chair. He spoke in a halting manner, the words fading away before the final syllable, as if he lacked the breath to complete them.

"I've come to ask you for my compositions," he said. "I have to leave, and I want to take them with me. If you've finished translating them, you know about a remarkable life, the tragic story of a wretch who drags himself painfully through pleasures only to destroy himself. If you haven't started . . ."

"I've almost finished it; I have just the last two pages that refer to your life in Brazil, if indeed it is you, the anguished figure who struggles in such an extraordinary narrative."

"Yes, it's me," he said. And turning pale, as if about to faint, continued in a somber voice, "There is little, almost nothing left, and that little bit is rather trivial. My life in Brazil . . . ! Here I have sought nature, I have only interacted with the landscape and the light; I have rested and now miss the earth and sky of this enchanting country. Impression . . . other than that of nature, I am left with only one. I got it from an unfortunate who enslaved herself to my shadow, who let herself get caught up in a dream . . . and died of love. I did with her what they say the mermaids do to the shipwrecked: while they are warm, they hold them in their arms, but as soon as they die and become cold, they reject them. I siphoned her feelings, I had her close to my soul like a sedative, I lived off that love. Perhaps it was spiritual vampirism."

"Miss Fanny?"

"That one. The most . . ."

"Are you leaving?"

"Yes, I'm leaving." He lowered his gaze, his body gently swayed, and his hair fluttered as if in a gust of wind. He buttoned up his coat.

"Where are you going?" My curiosity was piqued.

"I don't know. Give me the books." I put everything in a package and, handing it to him, felt the icy coldness of his fingers. I wanted to shake his hand, but shrinking back, he just nodded and turned away, leaving just as slowly as he had arrived.

I followed him to the top of the stairway and watched him go down, disappearing below. I could still hear his footsteps.

There was nothing extraordinary about the visit, yet I felt somehow haunted, loose in a void, unsettled and alone, very alone, abandoned, as if the entire silent house had been emptied of its inhabitants and was given over to obsessive spirits wandering vaguely through it. What could it be? My flesh shivered in annoying irritation, and my hair sprang up stiff on my head. For a moment I stood still, gazing in fear, seeing faint tiny flames that glowed mournfully before disappearing.

I went back to my room and sat smoking, looking out the open window at the calm and starry sky. "What was the matter with that man? What distressing haste compelled him to leave, with such hurried and silent steps?"

I shrugged my shoulders, trying to cast off the persistent thoughts that followed me like an obsession.

I thought I heard the door creak, crack, and open slowly, softly. I turned around quickly. There was nothing, just silence. Off in the neighborhood, the mournful sound of a piano could be heard amid the raucous automobile horns that bellowed in the distance.

Then I remembered the student who was waiting for me. I grabbed the folder where I'd kept my translation and, recalling the incredulous words he used when responding to my account, told myself, "Naturally he'll laugh when I tell him that James came to retrieve his originals and the mysterious book. Just when I needed to show them as proof, when I needed them to document my claim . . .

"But surely they saw him pass by as he left with the package. He wouldn't leave without saying goodbye to Miss Barkley . . ." And, without another thought, I went downstairs on my way to the cottage, carrying the folder.

VIII

Décio dozed lazily, stretched out on the divan, his arms folded under his head, lightly swaying his crossed legs. From the bronze incense burner perched atop the music stand came a thin aromatic thread of smoke. Sensing my presence, the student opened his eyes and quickly sat up as he looked at me, his countenance loosened in a smile.

"Did you bring the manuscript?"

"Part of it. The best part was taken just now by its owner."

"Who?" he cried in surprise. "The Englishman?"

"Yes."

"He was there?"

"For a minute."

"Then that's why Miss Barkley sent for our Orpheus."

"Brandt?"

"He's there with her. Alfredo carried him off just as he began playing a short prelude by Dukas."[47] He threw him-

47. Paul Dukas (1865–1935) was a French composer whose fame rests on a single orchestral work: *L'apprenti sorcier* (1897; *The Sorcerer's Apprentice*).

self heavily into the soft armchair and began to toy with the tassels of the armrest. Suddenly, he stood up, bursting into laughter:

"So, the Englishman made off with the mysterious book?"

"I give you my word . . ."

"That's incredible!" he exclaimed, laughing, squeezing my arm.

"You don't believe it . . . ?" I asked, annoyed.

He lit a cigarette and said, "He's really the sort of man who affects us deeply. If I had spent time with him as you did, I guarantee that I would have written a poem in rare verses, celebrating his beauty, grace, and Olympian strength."

"But you doubt what I tell you?"

"My dear man, truth is beauty. Who cares about its origin? You say it comes from that intelligent mind; so be it! But you must allow me to praise your modest genius. Sit down, open this folder, and delight me."

"I swear that this is nothing more than the work of a translator, and a bad one at that, and if I come to read this screed, with little value as to concept and form, it is because I feel there is a mystery in it. For you and for all who read it, it will never go beyond pure fantasy, but I got to know James, I listened to him and touched the scar on his body.

"Like Saint Thomas touched the scar of Christ . . . ?"

"Don't laugh. What need did this man have to pass himself off as a monster? Décio, his story was written with such painful sincerity that what impressed me most was not its wonder, but the suffering. The life of James Marian is, if not a mystery, madness disguised as melancholy."

"Perhaps."

"Do you believe in the science of the mahatmas?"

"Me? In matters of science, I question everything. Mahatmas?"

"Yes, those wise men of India who preserve, like a mystical fire, all that ancient wisdom that will yet shine in a new dawn."

"I don't know anything about that . . ."

"Well, my friend, either James is a madman, or his life is an absurd paradox, the lie embodied in the truth."

"Man, you speak with such conviction . . . What the devil! Is this serious?"

"My word of honor it is."

Décio got up, troubled, walking to the end of the room in measured steps before standing to contemplate the marble Venus de Milo, resplendent in the light. He gazed, enamored, at the divine white body and said, "This is also a mystery. All beauty is mysterious. And by the way—" He was fond of making puzzling, improvised transitions: "Do you know that I am anxiously looking for an Aphrodite, a perfect goddess, daughter of the white foam?" He fell silent, his eyes wide in ecstasy; and then continued thoughtfully, more slowly:

"My old man, there is nothing like water to preserve and give splendor to beauty. The bath, with fine soap and a drop of oil, is a ritual. Baptism's virtue lies in the washing. There is no better perfume than water: a clean body smells wonderful." He paused and then, brushing back his hair, exclaimed:

"That's what I find so enchanting about that diabolical woman—her clean smell. Because I don't know if you've ever noticed this—a washed body has every fragrance, like a garden . . . and water has no smell. White, not being a color, is the combination of all colors, just as water, since it is odorless, is the synthesis of all scents."

He took a deep breath and, with hands folded in adoration, praised the sea Venus: "Divine among the divinities!" Then, however, forgetting the goddess, he ran out the door to the garden and, in the shadow, under the branches of the flowering jasmine tree, murmured impatiently, "What's taking Brandt so long?" and in almost the same moment, exclaimed, throwing up his arms, "Here he comes!" And then, raising his voice, called out, "Hurry up! We're waiting at the threshold of mystery. Quicken that thoughtful step, man of rhapsody!"

And the artist answered calmly, in a laughing voice, "I'm coming."

The student stepped quickly forward to meet his friend and, linking arms, asked him, "What the devil did the Englishwoman want with you?" and, falling back into step, suddenly serious, with a gasping voice, "Do you know, sir, I'm beginning to suspect something in these nocturnal intimacies? Has the gentleman used sorcery to soften the hard heart of the monster?"

Brandt smiled. "Miss is always the same virtuous and prudent Minerva, friend of peace and order. She called me to suggest that I be a little more patient with the bookkeeper."

"Man, it's true . . . Today you were incensed! Your eyes looked like Zeus's Olympus, ignited by thunderbolts. So? Has the rascal been thrown out?"

"I don't know . . . He's impertinent, devilish: he irritates me. Just listening to him makes my nerves tingle. Instead of simply talking, he grates and yells. It's not anger I feel, it's impatience. I'm afraid of myself."

"Do you want my advice? Smash his face in."

Brandt sank into the divan, cracked his knuckles, and turned to me with a smile:

"Is it true, then, that you know the secret of James's life?"

"Yes, it's true."

"Astonishing, huh? A poem to be set to the music of Debussy?"[48]

"Perhaps."

He lazily stretched out his arm, removed a pipe from the tray, and filled it with tobacco before saying with regret, "I confess that I miss that fellow. And he left without a word, like a mute shadow. It was just now that Miss Barkley learned of his departure."

"Departure?"

"Yes, on the *Avon*, the day before yesterday."

I quickly stood up, dizzy, feeling a tingling sensation in every nerve. My voice came out hoarse, in a hiss, and I struggled to articulate my words. "He's gone? How? That's impossible."

"He left. At least that's what I heard from Smith, who was there with Miss Barkley, settling James's accounts."

Décio began whistling softly, looking around the room and, sensing my distress and naturally not wanting to embarrass me, walked straight toward the window and stood there, fiddling with the jasmine branch.

"No! That's impossible!" I insisted. "It's a joke!"

"Joke? I'm just repeating what I heard," said Brandt, unperturbed.

---

48. Claude Debussy (1862–1918) was a French composer of central importance in twentieth-century music.

"I'm telling you. I'm saying it's impossible. James was with me upstairs just fifteen minutes ago. He came to get a book he had loaned me and the originals I translated. I talked to him, walked him to the stairs . . ."

"You . . . ?"

"Yes, me." We looked at each other in silence. Brandt, with his keen eye, penetrating and direct, stared at my face, and I, embarrassed in front of the student who stood discreetly by the window, felt enveloped by a strange heat, as if my entire body were slowly catching fire. My blood pulsated in my arteries in fiery throbs, my eyes like hot coals. Suddenly, I was shaken by a violent tremor, and instantly a heavy shadow darkened the room, or my sight went dark with dizziness, but when brightness returned, I was near the piano, cold and shivering with agitation, and the two young men beside me seemed to be watching me, attentive and kind.

"What happened?" asked Décio, checking my pulse. I responded in a frantic shout, insisting on my allegation:

"It's impossible! James was with me a short time ago, he talked to me, asked for a book, the originals . . . It's impossible!"

Brandt was silent for a moment, his eyes downcast, stroking his mustache. Finally, as if uneasy, he said calmly, "If you want to find out for sure . . . Smith is probably still there with Miss Barkley. Let's go see."

I strode resolutely out to the garden, followed by the two young men. I moved as if in flight, not feeling the ground beneath my feet. The night air was cold, and I had a vague impression of rending fine mist.

Then suddenly, in a fit of vertigo, my head reverberated and seemed to grow, expanding and contracting with a constricting sensation of squeezing, threatening to burst, and everything inside me was hazy—my thoughts whirling, like dried leaves in a stormy gust of wind. I ran up the stairs.

Miss Barkley was talking to Smith on the veranda. When they saw us, they fell silent. Brandt, quieter, and forcing a laugh, apologized for interrupting their conversation, but wanted to "settle a matter" and asked the Englishman if it was true that James had left on the *Avon*.

"Yes, sir, he set off. I left him aboard."

As if struck by a brute force, I snapped at the Englishman.

"It's impossible!" Such an unexpected and violent denial caused him to spin around, facing me with a scowl, and Miss Barkley, no doubt surprised by my sharp response, intervened, confirming the words of her fellow countryman:

"Oh yes, he left on the *Avon*. Didn't you see his name on the passenger list?" I was stunned, and Brandt, to justify my amazement, explained to Smith that I had sworn that James Marian had been in my room just a short time ago.

"Oh!" said the Englishman, shuffling in his chair. "He's an eccentric one, that James. Oh! But appearing here when he is many miles away at sea, that . . ." Miss Barkley smiled, agreeing.

"And his baggage?" I asked.

"It was at my house in Tijuca. The little he had here my servant removed a few days ago. I have an order to sell the furniture he purchased here. The rest belongs to the house." And laughing, rubbing his hands in a slap on his thin thighs: "So you saw him?"

"As clear as I am seeing you now, sir. And besides that, I talked to him, handed him a book he had lent me and the originals of a novel."

"A book of scribbles and doodles? I saw that. He always carried it with him. It was stolen in Java, and he offered a thousand pounds to anyone who could get it back. They brought it to the hotel." And Smith, as if such a short story had tired him out, fell back into the wicker chair, stretched out his legs, and, with his head bowed down and hands clasped to his chest, concluded, "It is true . . . By this time, he should be somewhere near Bahia." He straightened up and, turning to Miss Barkley, picked up the thread of their conversation. Brandt then said goodbye.

"Thank you! Good night." Then the two went downstairs. I stood there, as if paralyzed.

"Aren't you coming?" the student asked from the garden. I made a vague gesture and hesitated a moment before looking up. Finally, slowly and weak-kneed, unnerved in a stupor of exhaustion, I walked toward the stairs and mindlessly headed up.

Upstairs, ragged, I breathed in large gulps of air, feeling a suffocating oppressiveness. The floor dissolved beneath my feet, the walls swayed, the ceiling arched, and the light, in a mortuary lividity far from bright, was opaque, giving me the impression of a yellow wall closing in on me—it was a light that immured me, a tomb's sinister twilight. Horrible!

Feeling my way, I instinctively reached the door of my room. Touching the door handle, it was as if I had activated an electric switch—the light cleared and shone brightly: I could see! But my ears were like deep, roaring caves, stormy thunder rumbled in my skull, and I was stunned with noises cascading down in a din, like waves crashing against a rugged shore.

I threw myself onto the divan, my frozen fingers squeezing my muddled head in distress. I could feel it grow, swelling up and bulging like a balloon, and from every corner of the room, mocking cackles whizzed through the air in ironic peals: it was a collective mockery;

uproarious jeering that riled me and filled me with great, unspeakable fear.

Oh! The fear! . . . It came in waves. I felt it coming and rising mightily, palpably, like the thick, dark waters of a raging flood. An itchy numbness tingled my feet that went cold and froze like stone.

The fear rose heavy to my knees, heavy and iron-like, encircling me in constricting rings, cinching my belly, splintering my chest, and causing my heart to beat frantically in anguish as if it were forcing its way through prison bars to escape. My throat constricted, and muscle spasms clenched my jaws; my labored breathing was raspy, like that of a dying man.

I stretched out on the divan, closed my eyes, and a ghostly vision flickered in the darkness: I saw dancing flecks of light; flashing, striped, snake-like shapes; a wild and confusing jumble of fire and darkness; sparks and licks of flames indiscriminately mixed with randomly shaped dark bodies, some curved, some long, some spherical, and some spirals.

I suddenly opened my eyes, terrified. I leaned against the edge of the divan, struggling to stand, but my energy was rendered useless in flaccid enervation, soft, as if I were steadying myself on folds of cotton.

Outside, so close! Life churned on. I heard voices, the whisper of carriages passing, the sound of piano; even the soft rustle of palm trees in the night air breathed heavy like a couple's panting. And I suffered.

As if lights began to be extinguished one by one inside me, I felt the darkness creep in, cold and mournful.

My mind was going dark like a city at dawn. Long avenues grew shadowy, cloudy, and deserted. I was at my end, it was my last day, my final hour, and I was dying, helplessly alone, with not even the ability to call out because I had no voice.

My eyes were powerfully drawn to the door, the door through which James, the ghost man, had entered and departed, and staring at it, I saw the entire wall dissolve into a starry background of sky, and below it, leaning against the ship's rail, his eyes locked on my face, was the beautiful and pale James Marian, wrapped in mysterious moonlight.

Despite the daze, I was thinking, reasoning and feeling that I was a victim of a hallucination. Because my sight was perfect, as clear as if it actually represented what was real. But no, it really was my room, and as I continued to stare, the scene slowly began to fade until it vanished; the wall reappeared, covering up the sky, and in place of the figure of the young man, and where he had stood, there now appeared a partially opened door. Only then did I realize that I was sitting down, my forehead dripping in sweat. I burned with the intense heat of fever, but my teeth chattered mightily.

Flashes of light alternated with the darkness like a storm cut by lightning; voices echoed in fuzzy whispers as the light-headedness returned and everything around me began to spin. I had the feeling of being sucked wildly into the air with the house, carried off as in a tornado.

I stretched out my hands to find support, standing up astonished, and managed to take a few off-balance steps before reaching the desk, and upon seeing my reflection in the mirror, my hair stood straight up in terror.

I summoned the courage to flee, but my movements were thwarted by a more powerful force. When I thought I had begun to move forward, I found myself in the very same spot, struggling uselessly.

I wept. Tears rolled down my cheeks, thick and silent.

Words formed in my head and came into my mouth only to recede without being uttered; even a scream beat and retreated like a ball rejected by a pediment. It was awful!

I was possessed, a victim of that succubus[49] demon whose bewitching machinations had wormed their way into my soul.

---

49. In folklore, a *succubus* is a demon or supernatural entity in female form that appears in dreams to seduce men, usually through sexual activity.

It was a demon, a real demon. Oh! I really felt it! . . . It had been there, just moments ago I had seen it, spoken to it, returned its things, while he was far away, across distant seas, making it impossible to physically communicate with me. How did he do that?

Sounds gently vibrated in the blessed silence, coming in through the open window in tender visitation to my soul, and as if by their melodious power, the fearful noises that had thunderously rattled me had died down, and I recognized Mendelssohn's "Wedding March."

It was Brandt who was playing, he, the amazing musician who had spoken up for me using his divine art, who was exorcizing the obsessing spirit.

And for a moment—a gentle and comforting moment!—I was at rest, listening and thinking, in the solitude of that haunted enclosure, so close to life yet so close to death.

I focused on the music, as if taking shelter in it. The sounds enveloped me, forming a veritable magical circle around me, and while the enchanting melody continued, the fear I could feel prowling around me was unable to reach me. I was like a galley slave who had loosened his shackles and eased his manacles—I could feel the irons but not their weight, nor the creasing and painful pressure. Suddenly, however, the silence became more muffled, and the visions and hallucinations began again.

Terrifying misgivings crept back into my mind, torturing me. Was it possible that a man who went so far away could manifest himself, in a real body, before my senses in real life? Was it possible?

I foolishly stood up quickly and, crazed and hurriedly, searched the desk for the mysterious book, the origins of the novel, but found only scribbled pages, with short notes, letters, and jotted notations.

Yet, just that morning I had consulted the book, and over the course of the day, as if guessing the unexpected outcome, I had worked on the translation without pause.

I stopped, tired and discouraged. My thoughts were muddled, ideas were confused, things from the past and from my childhood came to me mixed up with incidents from that day; recollections floated from the depths of my memory in a violent churning of my troubled mind, and my eyes, wide open and wild, saw not what was real, but rather bizarre chimeras: molded arabesques in space, discs, stripes, sparks, dazzling themselves in fascination or blinding themselves in the darkness.

The heat warmed me, swirling flames enveloped me, and then, in an abrupt transition, the cold chilled me to the point of impairment, rigidly covering my entire body as if I were shut away in an ice prison. I have a vague recollection of a struggle, of anxious figures hovering over me . . .

When I came back to life, what first impressed me was the white room in which I found myself, a room as bare as a monk's cell. Carefully following my every step was a man dressed all in white, wearing a cap and apron. Always attentive to my slightest beckoning, he would sit by my iron bed, and at night, I could feel him close, ever vigilant. Sometimes, when I opened my eyes in the sad twilight, I would see him, white and motionless, staring at me like a spirit.

It was not unusual in the silence of the night to hear the harrowing whine of a voice: screams, loud groans. I would shudder in terror, sitting up in bed, and soon the man would come to calm me, engaging me in conversation or silently smoking as he watched me.

Late one night, the entire house was roused in an agonized uproar. I jumped out of bed, listening: "Where am I? What hospital is this?" I asked the watchman who had come running. He grimaced disconcerted, without a ready response, saying only, "You're alright now. The director is going to discharge you." The uproar subsided, and the silence became more muffled and mournful.

Early the next morning, approaching the grated window of my room, I saw in the distance the sparkling city and blue sea, and below, at the far end of the garden and park, laborers were watering plots and patients were slowly wandering along a carpet of sun-speckled path in the sweetness of the fresh air. But from time to time, cries from the wards could be heard, the anguished and somber cries of those immured.

It was a hospital for the insane, the insane! And why was I there, observed by a doctor, watched over by a nurse, followed at every turn, with no freedom of movement, quickly surrounded like a dangerous beast if I strayed from my customary walk and took an uphill path through the hedges that led to the monstrous body of the quarry, which would at times rumble thunderously, shaking the houses with earthquake-like tremors? Why?

One morning, Décio came to visit. Not the happy, eloquent companion of yore but rather a restrained and circumspect young man, quietly affable, speaking to me in measured words, without the devil-may-care spurts of his playful genius.

He seemed to probe my soul before he entered it with his boisterous and unreserved cheerfulness, fearful perhaps of awakening what lay sleeping or of touching what was fragile.

He was the only friend I saw in that sad room, just him, no one else. And it was with him and my correspondent that, on a bright Sunday morning, at the festive ring of bells, I left my prison cell and that man in white, who at times seemed to emerge from the whitewashed walls like a grayish-white ghost, walking toward me without a whisper of a footstep, his gaze hard and fixed and his arms extended, a mournful figure.

My correspondent, showing me a letter from my mother in which the distressed woman had asked that I be sent to the homestead accompanied by a person of trust, put himself at my disposal, saying that if I wished, we could leave that night. I agreed. When getting into the carriage that awaited us at the door, casting one last look at the formidable gate of the house where I had lived, oblivious to the eclipse of my soul, I asked Décio, "So, I've been crazy . . . ?"

"Crazy? What craziness, man?" He looked at me, smiling, and as the carriage departed, he grabbed me tightly and said, with his typical cheerfulness and all the warmth of his joyful youth, "Neurasthenia,[50] my old man. Our neurasthenia! Do you want to know something? All of us, without exception, if surprised at certain points in time in such 'states of mind,' would have to spend some time in houses like this one. Don't think that this is only for the insane; it is also a refuge for those trapped in a fleeting storm of great dreams."

"And who doesn't have their little manias?" noted the correspondent.

---

50. *Neurasthenia* is a condition characterized by physical and mental exhaustion, usually accompanied by symptoms such as headache and irritability, and is often associated with depression or emotional stress.

"And my burst of madness was . . . James Marian?"

"Yes, the handsome Englishman."

"So it was a dream?"

"The existence of the man, no, he is real: the case of the book, his appearance that night . . . Do you remember?"

"Yes, I remember when he came to claim the book of his destiny and the originals of what he proposed was the story of his own life. I remember. They told me that such visit was impossible because he was . . ."

"Many leagues out at sea."

"But I assure you, I swear . . ." The correspondent cleared his throat, frowning at Décio.

I reassured him, affirming that I was in my right mind, and then went on to tell the student:

"If that's why they locked me up in that house, my dear Décio, I'm telling you that the alienists . . ."[51]

But the student interrupted me loudly: "Let's leave the past behind us. It was a crisis, a dive into the blue. Ah! My friend, the blue should be contemplated from afar, like this." And he leaned in, with a broad gesture indicating the clear, bright, luminous sky, shining in the sun.

---

51. *Alienist* likely originated from the French word *aliene*, meaning "insane," thus the noun *alieniste* (or *alienist* in English) referred to someone who treated the "insane." Starting around the mid–nineteenth century, those who studied and treated mentally ill patients were referred to as "alienists." In the early twentieth century the term was replaced by *psychiatrist* ("Alienist").

"It's a great day for a picnic," reminded the correspondent.

"With women!" added the student. The carriage rolled along.

I reentered life like a convalescent venturing out into the sun for the first time, feeling and enjoying all of nature's enchantments, partaking in the general cheer, seeing smiles and sadness, passing between fortune and misery, two lanes along the avenue of life. But the doubt, my God! Doubt that is to be my eternal companion, torturing doubt or, rather, the certainty that I will never prove to those who cast me off among the other crazy people, the truth of the incident of that afternoon, the horrible certainty of James Marian's visit, of his presence in my room, of his request for me to return the books and the originals, of his departure, of the whisper of his steps on the stairs . . . of all of it, all of it! That certainty, my God! . . . Madness?

No, I am perfectly calm, I can remember all the facts without omitting a single detail, I remember insignificant episodes . . . Yet if I mention everything, and if it's all true, then why should what affected me most deeply and what I remember most accurately be madness?

And now all who see me will say I'm crazy. Those days of confinement have rendered me useless for all time . . . and I'm certain that truth is with me: I saw it!

But who will take my word for it? Who?

Perhaps the ages will confirm what I say. The ages . . . !

When the day of truth dawns, who will remember the wretch who has passed?

Now I am branded like a galley slave: I was in an asylum.

How many innocents have been judged . . . ? How many, like me, have suffered for the truth? How many?

END

Works Cited in Footnotes

"Alienist, *N.*" *Online Etymology Dictionary*, 2001–22, www.etymonline.com/word/alienist.

"Bárbaro, *Adj.* (1)." *Michaelis*, 2022, michaelis.uol.com.br/moderno-portugues/busca/portugues-brasileiro/bárbaro.

"Brazil, the Regency." *Encyclopedia.com*, 2019, www.encyclopedia.com/humanities/encyclopedias-almanacs-transcripts-and-maps/brazil-regency.

"Charles Baudelaire's *Fleurs du mal / Flowers of Evil*." *Fleursdumal.org*, 2022, fleursdumal.org/poem/117.

Read, Ian Olivo. "Finding Fatalism and Overconfidence in a Cruel Port: The Bubonic Plague's First Appearance in Brazil." *Readex Report*, vol. 6, no. 2, Apr. 2011, www.readex.com/readex-report/issues/volume-6-issue-2/finding-fatalism-and-overconfidence-cruel-port-bubonic.

Sahoo, P. C. "Traditional Management of Occult Science." *Bulletin of the Deccan College Post-Graduate and Research Institute*, vols. 66–67, 2006–07, pp. 395–401. *JSTOR*, www.jstor.org/stable/42931464.

"Sophocles." *Britannica*, 17 Dec. 2022, www.britannica.com/biography/Sophocles.

"Theosophical Terms." *Blavatsky Archives*, www.blavatskyarchives.com/glossaryofexpandedterms.htm. Accessed 29 Dec. 2022.

"War of Canudos." *Wikipedia*, 21 Oct. 2022, en.wikipedia.org/wiki/War_of_Canudos.

Afterword: *Sphinx* Reconsidered

Jess Nevins

In retrospect it seems predictable that Henrique Maximiano Coelho Neto's *Sphinx* would be a critical failure when it was published in Brazil in 1908. The novel was a popular success with Brazilian readers and went through two more editions over the next twelve years, with a fourth edition appearing in Portugal in 1925, but Coelho Neto's many Brazilian critics thought little of it, and when the so-called first generation of Brazilian modernists denounced Coelho Neto and his oeuvre in the early 1920s, *Sphinx* was one of the examples they used. The reasons for the scorn, criticism, and abuse heaped on Coelho Neto by the first generation and its followers are numerous but can best be summarized as an assessment of Coelho Neto's work as bad writing and of Coelho Neto himself as the personification of everything that was wrong with Brazilian writing and the Brazilian literary establishment of the early 1920s.

The denunciation of *Sphinx* and the lingering contempt with which the post-1920s Brazilian literary establishment holds Coelho Neto was and is understandable in part; *Sphinx* is written in a florid, symbolist narrative style that was long out-of-date and that was repugnant to the aesthetic sensibilities of the first generation. But the deeper truth is that the first generation and the successive generations of Brazilian literary critics and academics who echoed its beliefs misunderstood *Sphinx*'s significance, ignored its radical content, and simply refused to properly situate the novel within its generic contexts. *Sphinx* was revolutionary within the genres it inhabited, both in Brazil and globally, and simultaneously represented an innovative summary of what had come before, an unusually accurate prediction of what was to come in certain genres, and a fascinating case of those genres that were wasting the potential of *Sphinx*'s example.

Sphinx can be concisely described as a Lusophone transgender *Frankenstein*,[1] but a broader description would include its presence in the genres of the gothic, horror, occult fantasy, and science fiction and its landmark status in the field of queer literature. *Sphinx* was not influential on those genres and fields; the novel was popular and was reprinted in 1912 and 1920, with a Portuguese edition following in 1925, but it was never translated for wider audiences, and, thanks to the scorn with which both it and Coelho Neto were held by the Brazilian literary establishment, the novel was quickly forgotten about in Brazil when the first generation took control of the Brazilian literary establishment. But *Sphinx* is nonetheless remarkable for its reification of ideas and movements that were mostly nebulous when it was written. It is also an intriguing case of what-if for some of the genres it inhabited.

Sphinx's greatest achievement is in the field of queer literature. By 1908 queer literature was well established globally, though such works appeared most often in covert form. *Sphinx* appeared during the first great flourishing of queer literature; the novel was published six years after André Gide's *L'Immoraliste* (*The Immoralist*), two years after Edward Prime-Stevenson's *Imre: A Memorandum*, four years before Thomas Mann's *Tod in Venedig* (*Death in Venice*), and five years before Marcel Proust's *À la recherche du temps perdu* (*In Search of Lost Time*). Brazilian readers had access to a small corpus of locally written queer works stretching back twenty years, beginning with Raul Pompeia's *O Ateneu* (*The Athenaeum*) and continuing through the early years of the twentieth century with the erotic magazine *Rio nu* (*Rio Naked*; Green 31–34) and the well-known literary work of the journalist, writer, playwright, and dandy João do Rio.

By 1908 queer literature in Brazil was associated with the naturalist movement and its approach to literature, to the degree that it can be said fairly that the emergence of homoerotic and gay-friendly fiction and drama was only possible because of the foundation provided by Brazilian naturalism. Writers like Aluísio Azevedo, Pompeia, Qorpo Santo, Nelson Rodrigues, and Oswald de Andrade had already written or were in the process of writing narratives and plays that dealt with homosexuality as a fixed category and used naturalism's observational approach to portray it (Bueno 393).

This means that *Sphinx* was not so much a setter of precedent or forerunner in the field of queer literature as it was an expression of a contemporary trend in Brazil. In 1908 the country was at the high point of its belle epoque, the sixteen-year period from 1898 to 1914 in which the culture of the social and economic elite of Rio de Janeiro "enjoyed [the city's] florescence" (Needell xi). The belle epoque was a reaction to the political and economic turmoil that had followed the abolition of slavery in 1888 and the declaration of the republic in 1889, a turmoil that had lasted until Manuel Ferraz de Campos Sales was named president in 1898 and the regional elites reasserted their power. Political, economic, and social stability followed, and culture, including literature, flowered.

The population of Rio de Janeiro also increased dramatically during the belle epoque, from 518,290 in 1890 to 800,000 by 1906 to 1,157,873 by 1920 (Green 17). While the number of native-born male *cariocas* (inhabitants of Rio de Janeiro) roughly matched the number of native-born female *cariocas*, the tens of thousands of Afro-Brazilians who poured into the capital in search of employment, and the tens of thousands of foreign immigrants who moved to Rio de Janeiro during the belle epoque, especially after the completion of its urban renovation project in 1906, were predominately male by a two-to-one margin (17–18). A significant number of these men sought out sexual experiences with other men, to the point that Rio de Janeiro, especially the Largo do Rossio square, gained a national reputation during the years of the belle epoque as a locus for homosexual behavior and gay culture. Homosexual subcultures had been present in Brazil long before the belle epoque; Luiz Mott mentions the "indigenous sexual culture . . . of the Tupinambá tribe" who greeted the Portuguese invaders (168). But the gay subculture of Rio de Janeiro during the belle epoque was seen as a new development.

Where *Sphinx* stands out from its contemporaries, and indeed from writers of queer literature around the world for at least the next twenty years, is in its sympathetic treatment of a transgender protagonist, James Marian, and in the novel's placement of Marian as the narrator's love interest. Before *Sphinx* there had been transgender characters in world literature—the creature in *Frankenstein* is a prominent example (Zigarovich)—as well as in Brazilian literature. But their creators had not treated them with compassion or as characters with agency. Joaquim Maria Machado de Assis's "As academias de Sião" ("The Academies of Siam"), the first Brazilian narrative with a transgender character, depicts a feminine king and a masculine concubine exchanging bodies (Ginway 42–45). But "As academias de Sião" is a fabular fantasy set in a fictional Asian country rather than in a homely and realistic Rio de Janeiro, as *Sphinx* is. Six years after *Sphinx*'s publication came Mário de Sá-Carneiro's *A confissão de Lúcio* (*The Confession of Lúcio*), a Portuguese novel that was widely distributed in Brazil. Sá-Carneiro's story uses bohemian Paris as a backdrop—another realistic setting, like *Sphinx*'s Rio de Janeiro—but the transgender character, Ricardo, is a narrative object rather than a subject and is eventually murdered by his lover, Lúcio, who cannot bear to admit to himself that his attraction to the male Ricardo is greater than his attraction to Marta, Ricardo's "alma, sendo sexualizada" ("sexualized soul"; 191; my trans.). Sá-Carneiro's deployment of the trope of the tragic queer individual in *The Confession of Lúcio* is some distance from James Marian's ultimately liberated destiny in *Sphinx*.

The main character of Coelho Neto's 1918 play *O patinho torto ou Os mistérios do sexo* (*The Twisted Duckling; or, The Mysteries of Sex*) is also transgender, but, like *Esfinge*, the critical reception to the play was muted. It would not be until the publication of Virginia Woolf's *Orlando* in 1928 that a novel with a major transgender character would portray that character in a sympathetic fashion. *Orlando* was also the first novel after *Sphinx* to be written by as well-known and popular an author as Coelho Neto was in 1908; although *Orlando* was a far greater international success than *Sphinx* was, *Sphinx* was more popular in Brazil than *Orlando* would later prove to be. For later writers of transgender fiction, *Orlando* was much more influential than *Sphinx*, which was forgotten about even in Brazil after 1930; but *Sphinx* has pride of place for its landmark positive portrayal of a transgender protagonist—*Orlando* was only available in Brazil as an English-language import from Portugal until 1945.

Like Coelho Neto's life and work, portrayals of transgender characters and indeed queer characters as a whole took a turn for the worse beginning in 1922,[2] when the Semana de Arte Moderna (Modern Art Week) took place 10–17 February in São Paulo. The Modern Art Week marked the formal introduction of modernism to Brazil and was a watershed moment both for Brazilian literature and for Coelho Neto's reputation and standing. Coelho Neto, a Parnassian poet and symbolist, was wholly opposed to the nascent modernism of what came to be called the first generation of Brazilian modernist writers, and the first-generation writers were in turn scornful of Coelho Neto, of his literary style, of his voluminous output, and of his standing in the society of writers in the capital. The first generation was also scornful of queer fiction: what had been a period of visibility of fictional homoerotic desire and gender transgressiveness disappeared in 1922 after the Semana de Arte Moderna: "During the *Geração Heróica* ["heroic generation," the poets, critics, and writers who made their names during the Semana de Arte Moderna], the concerns with the vanguards and 'isms' coming from Europe as well as their appropriation and *deglutição* ["swallowing"] into something new became an issue for the Modernists" (Nemi Neto 17–18).

Sphinx, then, represents a wasted opportunity for Brazilian fiction and international fiction. After the minor flourishing of transgender literature in the early- and mid-1920s (Taylor 209), which culminated in Woolf's *Orlando*, transgender fiction was shunned for decades: the first major post-*Orlando* work of fiction with a transgender protagonist, Gore Vidal's *Myra Breckenridge*, was not published until 1968, and after *Sphinx*, the first Brazilian work of fiction with a transgender protagonist, André Carneiro's "Transplante de cérebro" ("Brain Transplant"), did not appear until 1978. The example that *Sphinx* set, that of a sympathetic transgender protagonist and love interest, was quickly avoided by other writers and then forgotten about, and sympathetic transgender characters would not become protagonists in a regular fashion until the twenty-first century.

Coelho Neto's Latin American contemporaries, though they were accomplished writers who wrote memorable and even brilliant works of gothic fiction and horror, did not manage to cross genres as ably as Coelho Neto did, nor did their works usually overcome their innately conservative tendencies toward gender and sex. In Chile, gothic fiction of the nineteenth century combined traditional gothic tropes, motifs, and plot devices with material unique to Chilean society, culture, and history: authors like Benjamín Vicuña Mackenna, Francisco Ulloa, and Joaquín Díaz Garcés wrote gothic novels about the search for origins and about the past coming back to haunt the present but used settings like crumbling and haunted haciendas, characters like bandits from the rural areas of Chile, and themes such as the search for buried treasure in the form of Spanish coins from the years of colonization (Ries 28–31).

In Brazil, Machado de Assis was the giant of Brazilian gothic horror stories in the second half of the nineteenth century and the early years of the twentieth century. But Machado de Assis's horror fiction was only one-tenth of his total output (Nevins, *Horror Needs No Passport* 10), and his horror stories tended toward the satirical or allegorical. His stories do condemn patriarchal ideology and the oppression of women (Jones and Krause 72), but they do not come close to approaching the subject of gender instability, much less transgenderism. Coelho Neto would have viewed Machado de Assis with respect—Machado de Assis was famous and respected throughout Latin America—but though the two were contemporaries, they wrote very different types of fiction.

In Honduras, authors like Froylán Turcios, Rubén Darío, Leopoldo Lugones, Clemente Palma, and Fabio Fiallo were part of the modernist movement, which held sway in Honduras for more than a decade before it reached its peak with the Modern Art Week in São Paulo in 1922. These writers, among the most famous of the Honduran *modernistas*, embraced modernism's faith in the existence of magical and supernatural events and beings that

> existed outside the realm of science and rational thought. . . . [T]he *modernista* vampires and doubles embodied excess, mystery, contradictions, and the impossible. These monsters thus destabilized reason, and represented the return of the repressed, the monstrous, and the Devil himself—all that could never fully be understood or tethered—that conveyed a heightened appreciation for mystery and wonder, to which the *modernistas* were clearly drawn. (Serrano 73)

The work of these writers, as *modernistas*, was opposed in many ways to that of the Parnassian Coelho Neto.

In Brazil, the "literatura do inusitado" ("literature of the unusual"; Abraham 717; my trans.), a category that includes Coelho Neto's work, was, contrary to traditional literary histories, very popular with readers, much more so than the work of authors of high art (Quereilhac 155). Popular authors like Eduardo Ladislao Holmberg, Lugones, and the Uruguayan Horacio Quiroga were Coelho Neto's acknowledged contemporaries. Yet Holmberg's work tended toward the science fictional, Lugones "specialized in de Maupassant–like *contes cruel*" (Nevins, *Horror Needs No Passport* 9),[3] and Quiroga's area of expertise was in Kipling-like fiction set in the wilderness of the rain forest. Again, Coelho Neto's exploration of gender instability and transgenderism were quite unlike that which his contemporaries were producing.

Other genres and the writers associated with them similarly wasted the opportunity presented by Coelho Neto and *Sphinx*. Certainly, the genres of fantasy, the gothic, horror, occult fantasy, and science fiction, which are central parts of the field known as *fantastika*[4] and which *Sphinx* represents in equal quantities, could have produced groundbreaking work by following *Sphinx*'s example. But they did not, to the detriment of each genre.

Science fiction as a distinct genre was well established by 1908. The best works of Jules Verne and H. G. Wells had already been published, and numerous other writers, less remembered now but notable in their day—from Max Pemberton in England to Camille Flammarion in France to Cândido de Figueiredo in Portugal—were producing science fiction. These science fiction novels and collections were available in Brazil through imports from Portugal, and Coelho Neto was an "avid" reader of them (Brito). Brazilian authors had been publishing science fiction from the mid–nineteenth century (Molina-Gavilán et al. 380), and gothic science fiction was flourishing in Brazil when Coelho Neto wrote *Sphinx*. Gothic science fiction can be defined as a type of fiction that makes use of the plots, characters, and devices of science fiction but avoids the logic, verisimilitude, and scientific plausibility of most science fiction of the time, instead putting those plots, characters, and devices at the service of bizarre, grotesque, fantastic situations (Tavares 15)—an apt description of *Sphinx*.

Yet for all the variety of science fiction in 1908, the works in the genre were in some ways severely limited. It's true that, as Peter Nicholls says, the period between 1895, when Wells began publishing his science fiction, and 1926 were "considerably more packed [with science fiction] than even 1863–1895." But with the very rare exception of obscurities like Gregory Casparian's *The Anglo-American Alliance*, science fiction, whether American or international, was not progressive on queer issues, nor was its treatment of gender issues or women much better. What is traditionally called *soft science fiction*, or science fiction that emphasizes feelings and relationships rather than science and technology, is generally assumed by critics to have begun deliberately with the work of Wells in the 1890s and early 1900s. Certainly Wells was a prime influence on many science fiction writers during those two decades. But a close examination of the science fiction stories and novels he published between 1895 and 1908 shows that the major concerns of the great majority of the texts were technological, sociological, or action-adventure entertainment, and emotions and relationships were treated as much less important, if not as afterthoughts. *Sphinx*'s focus on the narrator's confused feelings for James Marian and on Marian's emotions and psychological well-being was a rarity, but it was also a preview of the direction mainstream science fiction would begin to take forty years later. Had *Sphinx* become widely read and popular in the United States, it may well have created an opportunity for science fiction writers to avoid the puerilities so common in the pulp science fiction of the 1920s, 1930s, and early 1940s and instead to match the development of the mystery genre, science fiction's better-accepted and more advanced sibling.

Gothic fiction, whether mimetic or fantastic, had been appearing in Brazil since 1843 (Menon, *Figurações* 92), and at the end of the nineteenth century and the beginning of the twentieth century, its subgenre, gothic science fiction, was particularly popular with Brazilian readers. This was especially true in Rio de Janeiro, where the influx of new technology—the electric tram, the telegraph, the telephone, X-rays, the automobile, the airplane, and the various seemingly fantastic goods advertised daily in the newspapers, among many others (El Far 120)—and the circumscribed rationalism of the Brazilian ruling class led to Brazilian readers demonstrating "um misto de fascinação e temor em relação ao progresso e a ciência da *Belle Époque*" ("a mixture of fascination and fear in relation to the progress and science of the belle epoque") that became the "matéria prima" ("raw material") for a comparatively large number of Brazilian gothic science fiction narratives in the 1890s and 1900s (Silva 267; my trans.).

Brazilian writers' heavy use of the gothic was similar to that of their English and European counterparts, who had made the so-called gothic revival one of the dominant forms of fiction in the 1890s and 1900s. These gothic revival novels, also referred to as neo-gothic novels, included Robert Louis Stevenson's *Dr. Jekyll and Mr. Hyde*, Oscar Wilde's *The Picture of Dorian Gray*, Arthur Machen's *The Great God Pan*, Wells's *The Island of Doctor Moreau*, Richard Marsh's *The Beetle*, and Bram Stoker's *Dracula*. It is true that the concerns of European and English gothic revival authors were quite different from those of Brazilian writers; European and English gothic writers emphasized themes of spiritual, physical, and racial degeneration as well as the threat of immigration, while Brazilian gothic authors produced works that grappled with Brazilian concerns, specifically for Brazilian audiences.

Sphinx was published during a time when writers in Europe and England were shifting from neo-gothic novels to more overtly horrific short stories (Killeen 161). In Brazil, *Sphinx* was the last of the novel-length gothic narratives that had been published since the 1820s, and after 1908, there was a return to shorter narratives (Menon, "Questão"). *Sphinx* stands out among the neo-gothic novels of the 1900s in a number of ways: the bizarre, grotesque, and fantastic situations of the novel's story, which are stereotypical of gothic fiction (Tavares 15); the similarities between the novel and

Joris-Karl Huysmans's *À rebours* (*Against Nature*), especially when one recalls that "o desvio sexual e a sensação de perversão moral que James provoca inadvertidamente nas pessoas ao seu redor se constitui como uma das características não apenas do Decadentismo . . . mas também da própria literatura gótica do período" ("the sexual deviance and the sense of moral perversion that James inadvertently causes in the people around him constitutes one of the characteristics not only of decadentism . . . but also of gothic literature of the period"; Silva 269; my trans.); and the many ways in which *Sphinx* fulfills the definitions of the gothic provided by Fred Botting:

> *Gothic* condenses the many perceived threats to these [social and moral] values, threats associated with supernatural and natural forces, imaginative excesses and delusions, religious and human evils, social transgression, mental disintegration and spiritual corruption. If it is not a purely negative term, Gothic writing remains fascinated by objects and practices that are constructed as negative, irrational, immoral and fantastic. . . . Gothic excesses, none the less, the fascination with transgression and anxiety over cultural limits and boundaries, continue to produce ambivalent emotions and meanings in their tales of darkness, desire and power. (1)

More gothic texts would appear after 1908, but most of them were short stories or were published in *folhetins*, or pamphlets, and Coelho Neto was responsible for a large percentage of them (Menon, "Questão"). The first generation scorned the gothic as insufficiently modern and was happy to let it dwindle and die.

Sphinx is equal parts science fiction and occult fantasy. *Occult fantasy* is fiction in which the protagonists pursue hidden knowledge or secret doctrine, regardless of the danger posed by the bearers of that knowledge or doctrine, in search of a moment of mystic revelation or transcendence (Ashley 702). The narrator's quest for the truth about James Marian, James Marian's quest for the truth about himself, and the figure of Arhat, the Asian mystic who is a kind of mentor to Marian, place *Sphinx* in the occult fantasy category. In 1908 occult fantasy was flourishing in Europe and England, having first appeared in the mid–nineteenth century in the works of Lord Bulwer-Lytton and later in theosophical fantasies inspired by Madame Blavatsky and in works such as Ignatius Donnelly's *Atlantis: The Antediluvian World*, Huysmans's *À rebours*, W. Somerset Maugham's *The Magician*, and stories and novels from writers as varied as Machen, Algernon Blackwood, and M. R. James.

In Brazil, however, occult fantasy was virtually nonexistent. The Brazilian reading audience was familiar with Blavatsky's theosophical writings, the basis of the modern occult fantasy genre, thanks to an 1892 Portuguese translation of Blavatsky's *Theosophical Glossary*, but neither the prevailing literary culture nor the audience's expectations would allow for occult fantasy as a fully realized literary genre. In 1908 Brazil, fantasy fiction was influenced by the Byronic tales of Manuel Antônio Álvares de Azevedo's *Noite na taverna* (*A Night in the Tavern*) or were utopias like Emília Freitas's *A rainha do Ignoto* (*The Queen of the Unknown*); it was not influenced nor allowed to be influenced by Blavatsky's philosophy. (Bulwer-Lytton's landmark 1842 theosophist fantasy, *Zanoni*, was not published in Brazil until 1988.)

Sphinx therefore should have been a groundbreaking work in Brazil. And its publication in Portugal in 1925 should have signaled to European readers that it was possible to meld the concerns of occult fantasy with issues of gender and sexuality and with a non-European, non-English, and non-American setting and cast of characters—all of which English and European occult fantasies of the era signally failed to do. But *Sphinx* appeared without garnering much recognition in Portugal and did not inspire imitators in Brazil. In the case of Brazil, it may be that, before Modern Art Week, *Sphinx*'s occult fantasy elements were too much at odds with the country's Catholicism and that, after Modern Art Week, the modernists' disdain for popular genre works of fiction led possible imitators of Coelho Neto to choose other writers to emulate. For Europe and England, *Sphinx* was too different from the theosophical occult fantasies that readers and writers were used to, insufficiently bent the knee to Blavatsky and theosophy, and incorporated a transgender protagonist in ways that neither Europe nor England were prepared to accept.

Sphinx can be described not only as a work of science fiction and occult fantasy but also as a work of horror. In England and Europe, the horror genre was well into its golden age by 1908: works by Machen, Blackwood, Lord Dunsany, and James had revolutionized horror fiction over the previous fifteen years and provided countless writers with inspiration to create fear-generating fiction in ways unbound by Victorian assumptions and limitations. In Brazil, horror fiction was beginning to appear on a regular basis. Azevedo's 1878 *Noite na taverna* is generally seen as the first major work of Brazilian horror fiction; by 1908 a number of stories by Machado de Assis and João do Rio had appeared, as had numerous stories in newspapers modeled on the work of Edgar Allan Poe or the French *conte cruel* (Nevins, *Horror Fiction* 59).

Certainly, *Sphinx* has its fear-inducing moments; as Andressa Silva Sousa and Emanoel Cesar Pires de Assis note, the progression of the story destabilizes the reader's sense of reality, and the reader's natural identification with the narrator leads to the reader, like the narrator and Miss Fanny, being unnerved by the apparently supernatural appearances of James Marian when he is supposed to be elsewhere (155–56). As Roberto de Sousa Causo points out, "Cada cénario é montado com cuidado, o grau de sobrenatural de cada evento fantástico é calculado para amparar o suspense, e os diálogos contribuem para a caracterização dos personagens, dando a cada uma voz própria" ("Each scenario is carefully assembled, the degree of supernaturalness of each fantastic event is calculated to support the suspense, and the dialogues contribute to the characterization of the characters, giving each one their own voice"; 113; my trans.). And Menon usefully notes both the influence of *Frankenstein* and the use of the gothic doppelgänger in *Sphinx* ("Questão").

Yet *Sphinx*'s focus on the reality of Marian's gender, on transgenderism itself, and on the seemingly romantic plot development was at odds with the horror fiction of the time, both in Europe and in Brazil, and *Sphinx*'s relegation of its terrifying moments to secondary status—*Sphinx* can be described as a work of horror, but the emphasis of the novel is on producing affects in the reader aside from fear and horror—was rare in European and Brazilian horror.

Sphinx could have led horror fiction writers by example; the novel's transgender love interest, its consideration of the true nature of transgender individuals, and its mosaic-like assemblage of affect-causing elements could have been the model for further horror narratives. But Brazilian horror after 1908 ignored *Sphinx* and continued to work in the modes of Poe or the *conte cruel*, and after the Modern Art Week horror fiction would virtually disappear from Brazilian bookshelves, only reappearing after the end of World War II in the works of writers like Graciliano Ramos and João

Guimarães Rosa (Nevins, *Horror Needs No Passport* 81–82). Likewise, European and English horror writers followed the prevailing trends in fiction, making their horror more pulpish or mainstream, then more concerned with fascism, communism, or small towns and suburbs; the elements that made *Sphinx* successful as horror fiction were ignored.

The time has come for a widespread critical reevaluation of *Sphinx*. It is a remarkable novel that adroitly combines science fiction and gothic horror while sympathetically, and presciently, portraying transgender and gay characters. These elements were individually seen in the work of other authors before Coelho Neto took hold of them, but not in a cohesive narrative that combines a lapidary narrative style with the breach of genre barriers. *Sphinx* deserves revisiting and rediscovery as a work significantly ahead of its time, both in Brazil and around the world.

Notes

1. My choice of the term *transgender* to describe James Marian is based on Marian's transition from two beings (a sister and a brother) to one being with two souls (one female, one male) to a being that is female ("é minha irmã a vitoriosa em mim" ["my sister is the victor in me"; ch. 6]). If gender identity is a person's inner sense of being male, female, both, or neither, then being transgender means that a person's inner sense of self is at odds with the gender role assigned to them by family, friends, and society. I view James Marian as transgender because of Marian's transition from both male and female to female and because Marian's gender identity is at odds with externally imposed gender roles.

2. Although Coelho Neto's works continued to sell well through the 1920s, he was held in critical disrepute, and after his death in 1934, he quickly became an author who, when remembered in Brazil at all, was remembered with scorn. A revival of interest in his work in Brazil only occurred in the twenty-first century.

3. The *conte cruel* ("cruel tale") was a short story genre, popular in the nineteenth and early twentieth centuries, that contained cruel climac-

tic twists and emphasized the irony of fate. Guy de Maupassant (1850–93) was a noted French practitioner of the form.

4. *Fantastika*, as developed and used by the critic John Clute, is a term encompassing all literature that contains the fantastic, including but not limited to science fiction, fantasy, fantastic horror, and all their various subgenres ("Fantastika").

Works Cited

Abraham, Carlos. *La literatura fantástica argentina en el siglo XIX*. Ciccus, 2015.

Ashley, Mike. "Occult Fantasy." *Encyclopedia of Fantasy*, edited by John Clute and John Grant, St. Martin's Press, 1997, pp. 702–04.

Botting, Fred. *Gothic*. Routledge, 1995. The New Critical Idiom.

Brito, Dayane. "A relação homem-ciência no Brasil da Belle Époque: Uma análise de *Esfinge*, de Coelho Neto." II Internacional de Narrativa Fantastica, 22 Oct. 2015, Raul Porras Barrenechea Institute, La Victoria, Peru. *Academia.edu*, 2022, www.academia.edu/32707065.

Bueno, Eva Paulino. "Brazilian Naturalism and the Politics of Origins." *MLN*, Mar. 1992, pp. 363–95.

Casanova-Vizcaíno, Sandra, and Inés Ordiz, editors. *Latin American Gothic in Literature and Culture*. Routledge, 2018.

Causo, Roberto de Sousa. *Ficção científica, fantasia e horror no Brasil, 1875–1950*. Editora UFMG, 2003.

El Far, Alessandra. *Paginas de sensacao: Literatura popular e pornografico no Rio de Janeiro, 1870–1924*. Companhia das Letras, 2004.

"Fantastika." *SFE: The Encyclopedia of Science Fiction*, 7 Nov. 2022, sf-encyclopedia.com/entry/fantastika.

Ginway, Mary Elizabeth. "Transgendering in Luso-Brazilian Speculative Fiction from Machado de Assis to the Present." *Luso-Brazilian Review*, vol. 47, no. 1, 2010, pp. 40–60.

Green, James N. *Beyond Carnival: Male Homosexuality in Twentieth-Century Brazil*. U of Chicago P, 1999.

Jones, Jordan B., and James R. Krause. "The Femme Fragile and Femme Fatale in the Fantastic Fiction of Machado de Assis." *Revista abusões*, vol. 1, no. 1, 2016, pp. 51–97.

Killeen, Jarlath. *Gothic Literature, 1825–1914*. U of Wales, 2009.

Menon, Maurício Cesar. *Figurações do gótica e de seus desmembramentos na literatura brasileira de 1843 a 1932*. 2007. Universidade Estaduel de Londrina, PhD dissertation.

———. "A questão do duplo em duas narrativas brasileiras." I Colóquio Internacional de Estudos Linguísticos e Literários, 10 June 2010, Universidade Estadual de Maringá.

Molina-Gavilán, Yolanda, et al. "Chronology of Latin American Science Fiction, 1775–2005." *Science Fiction Studies*, vol. 34, no. 3, Nov. 2007, pp. 369–431.

Mott, Luiz. "Crypt-Sodomites in Colonial Brazil." *Infamous Desire: Male Homosexuality in Colonial Latin America*, edited by Pete Sigal, U of Chicago P, 2003, pp. 168–96.

Needell, Jeffrey. *A Tropical Belle Epoque: Elite Culture and Society in Turn-of-the-Century Rio de Janeiro*. Cambridge UP, 2009.

Nemi Neto, João. *Anthropophagic Queer: A Study on Abjected Bodies and Brazilian Queer Theory in Literature and Film*. 2015. City U of New York, PhD dissertation.

Nevins, Jess. *Horror Fiction in the Twentieth Century: Exploring Literature's Most Chilling Genre*. Praeger, 2020.

———. *Horror Needs No Passport: Twentieth Century Horror Literature outside the U.S. and U.K.* 2018.

Nicholls, Peter. "History of SF." *SFE: The Encyclopedia of Science Fiction*, 21 May 2021, www.sf-encyclopedia.com/entry/history_of_sf/.

Quereilhac, Soledad. "Shadows of Science in the Río de la Plata Turn-of-the-Century Gothic." Casanova-Vizcaíno and Ordiz, pp. 155–71.

Ries, Olga. "Rural Horrors in Chilean Gothic." Casanova-Vizcaíno and Ordiz, pp. 27–40.

Sá-Carneiro, Mário de. *A confissão de Lúcio, narrativa*. Em casa de autor, 1914.

Serrano, Carmen. "Duplicitous Vampires Annihilating Tradition and Destroying Beauty in Froylán Turcios's *El vampiro*." Casanova-Vizcaíno and Ordiz, pp. 71–83.

Silva, Alexander Meireles da. "O admirável mundo novo da República Velha: O nascimento da ficção científica brasileira." *Eutomia: Revista de literatura e linguística*, Dec. 2008, pp. 262–83.

Sousa, Andressa Silva, and Emanoel Cesar Pires de Assis. "'Efeito de real' versus sobrenatural: Um conflito necessário à construção da fantasticidade em *Esfinge*, de Coelho Neto." *Revista da letras*, July 2017, pp. 144–61.

Tavares, Braulio. "Nas periferias do real ou, O fantástico e seus arredores." *Páginas de sombra: Contos fantásticos brasileiros*, edited by Tavares, Casa da Palavra, 2003, pp. 7–19.

Taylor, Melanie. "True Stories: *Orlando*, Life-Writing, and Transgender Narratives." *Modernist Sexualities*, edited by Hugh Stevens and Caroline Howlett, Manchester UP, 2000, pp. 202–18.

Zigarovich, Jolene. "The Trans Legacy of *Frankenstein*." *Science Fiction Studies*, vol. 45, no. 2, July 2018, pp. 260–72.

About the Contributors

Kim F. Olson is a Portuguese-language translator and editor. A lover of foreign languages since childhood, she received a BS in Portuguese from Georgetown University before earning a BA in translation from the Pontifical Catholic University of Rio de Janeiro. Her work as a freelancer, which spans over thirty years, includes several recent forays into the literary realm. *Sphinx* is her second book-length literary translation.

M. Elizabeth Ginway is professor of Spanish and Portuguese studies at the University of Florida, where she teaches courses on Portuguese language, Brazilian literature and culture, and Latin American science fiction. Her most recent book is *Cyborgs, Sexuality, and the Undead: The Body in Mexican and Brazilian Speculative Fiction* (2020).

Jess Nevins is a librarian at Lone Star College, Tomball. He is the author of multiple works on popular fiction and literary history, including *Horror Fiction in the Twentieth Century* (2020), *The Evolution of the Costumed Avenger* (2017), and *The Victorian Bookshelf: An Introduction to Sixty-One Essential Novels* (2016).